Plugging the Causal Breach

and other stories

Mary Byrne

Regal House Publishing

Published by
Regal House Publishing, LLC
Raleigh, NC 27612
All rights reserved

Printed in the United States of America

ISBN -13 (paperback): 9781947548718
ISBN -13 (epub): 9781947548725
ISBN -13 (mobi): 9781947548732
Library of Congress Control Number: 2019938901

Interior and cover design by Lafayette & Greene
lafayetteandgreene.com
Cover images © by frankie's/Shutterstock

Regal House Publishing, LLC
https://regalhousepublishing.com

For France, which has put up with me for quite a long time

and
in memory of

Jean-Claude (who remained strong and silent throughout)
my mother (who taught me to read)
my father (who carried reading material home in his pocket
on the bicycle)

CONTENTS

Au Pair Girls Wanted in France

He drove me into the town, moving a parcel of meat to the floor at his feet, out of my way.

'I do live in Machaire Rua,' he said, as if he only did it sometimes. We passed rusting signs in English and Irish for small towns and villages, and sometimes for deer, or winter-neglected forest parks and picnic areas. Along the roadside new houses with porches and pillars had sprung up, modelled on houses in other countries. He seemed impressed by them.

'The brick is warmer than the concrete,' he said.

We got talking of the long darkness before Christmas. He liked it as little as I did.

'You can't go out without getting covered in muck,' he said.

At the hotel, it was lunchtime, and what sounded like an instrumental *Ave Maria* was coming over the intercom. In the lounge, two girls tucked into their soup, leaning over low tables, carefully eyeing two identical girls who had also come for soup, which would be followed by sandwiches, and tea. These girls ate the same fare every day.

The theme from *Exodus* came over the intercom.

In the next booth, three voices: 'She went off—did the interview and went off to Saudi, after marrying an Englishman she met on holidays.'

'I wouldn't go near Saudi,' said a second voice, 'the culture is so different.'

1

'My friend went—I told her she was mad.'

'I personally would have nothing to do with one of those guys.'

'Yes,' said a third, 'they could be married or anything, they're not like ourselves.'

'Sure you couldn't go nowhere out there.'

Over the top of the booth, the hairstyles of the three (girls? women?)—and the heads—looked like those of men.

Suddenly the pipe exuded music that suggested a continental forest, and a woman in designer clothes— perhaps a fur coat and hat—walking in snow.

The girls across the way were on their sandwiches. New girls arrived, wearing shirts and light trousers at half mast, showing a length of cold leg and ankle. They were not wearing coats, had no coats with them.

'How are ye,' they said—rather than asked—those already eating. 'Not too bad,' came the answer, as if from old and weary women. All of them huddled their light-clad shoulders against the cold, already taking on the shape of toil-worn grannies.

'Nothing only tomato soup left,' the new arrivals said, 'wouldn't you know it!'

'I wish I was in Carrickfergus', warbled in the background. The girls were joined by one of the waitresses who dipped into the local newspaper with them.

In one part of the bar it was daylight, in another night, with subdued lighting under frilly red shades. On one wall hung an aerial photo of the town's main street: white building, grey slate roofs, multi-colored cars at right angles.

Near me the blue velvet seating had a cigarette burn,

and further along the seat a whole square had been cut out: drunken revels? souvenir? plans for a patch? 'The Green Glens of Antrim', played, bringing with it memories of the 1950s.

In the booth, the topic had changed: 'I was shocked—' 'Tragic.'

'I couldn't get over it. I was only, I'd say, about ten at the time.'

'Oh stop.'

Thirty minutes to go. I walked up the main street. In a window, a sign said 'Au pair girls wanted in France, Germany, Italy, Belgium, Holland, Canada.' Next door, a Christian Fellowship window had its Bible open at Hosea, with a sentence underlined: 'For the land hath committed great whoredom, departing from the Lord.'

A bright blue parrot of synthetic fur sat in a glass cage outside a sweetshop, inscribed, 'A prize every time.' Occasionally it burst into speech: 'Who's a pretty boy then?' and, after an interval, 'I love the sound of money.'

Nearly time. Back in the hotel lobby, it was early afternoon and the TV was functioning loudly: 'Don't call the police, honey, save your dime for the kid's father.' The heroines looked like men in drag, with bouffant hair and thick make-up. They wore, at work and on the street, dresses that would be risqué in any circumstances. A young man near me sighed hopelessly.

It was time. A scattering of people began to collect at the hotel door.

'It's dead.' The young man was here too. He was not speaking to anyone in particular. He looked down the main street: 'These places are dead. But then Dublin is no great shakes either.'

And finally the bus came, and no word was spoken as we all mounted the vehicle which was lined with carpet. On the windscreen fluttered a selection of small plastic flags from different countries.

We moved off, under grey skies and around green hills. Every peak was a ring fort in which were hiding na Tuatha de Danann and na Sidhe, waiting for better times.

Outside the town a late passenger boarded, waved off by an old lady with white hair.

'Lovely day,' the passenger said.

'Great,' the driver replied, keeping his eye on the road.

RTE Radio 2 rattled overhead, neither soft enough to be ignored nor loud enough to be heard properly. Wrong answers to a quiz filtered through.

'What's a marsupial?' the presenter asked.

'A squid,' replied the caller.

'Who built Hadrian's Wall?'

'The Chinese.'

We passed a sign declaring 'Bull calves for sale,' and a man paused from his gardening to gaze over his hedge at us. In one of the towns, a bakery door announced 'Birthday cakes always in stock.' It would be my birthday soon. I was leaving this landscape where I had spent all of my years. And we had just passed a house modelled on Dallas's South Fork.

What Doesn't Choke Will Fatten

I bought *escalopes de dinde* for the four of us, as per Marguerite's instructions. She likes stuff that's easy to cook and easy to eat for people who haven't much left to chew with.

The butcher's fat brother sat in the little kiosk dividing the mouth of the shop in two. He was wearing his white coat over a big pullover.

'Cold enough for you?' he enquired. 'They say it'll get worse and stay like that for weeks.'

'No one's making you sit out here,' I said. 'Go back where it's heated; maybe do a little work with that brother of yours. What makes you such a traditionalist?'

'Happy New Year to you too,' he said.

When I got home, Marguerite was talking about the weather too.

'Cold is forecast. Check all doors and walls—the rodents will come knocking tonight,' she said.

'Night of the long tails,' I said.

'Enough,' said Marguerite.

It was that kind of season. The cat thickened up his fur.

On days like these I test whether I am still capable of pity. There are plenty of opportunities. Last night a man died of cold in Grenoble.

Pretending he had a night job, he was sitting in his car all night. Welcome to the new France. I try to compare minus 5°C with the minus 30°C that winter of '42, but I can only relate it to concrete things like food and toes and the injured hand that made me walking wounded and worth saving. I remember the doctor, an Austrian, but not the pain. The body doesn't want to remember. We all ended up in France. The Austrian was later billeted with a family in the south. He got the girl of the house pregnant and stayed forever.

It was getting near lunchtime when Denis walked in with this specimen I knew was wrong from the start. Denis was smiling and talking too much, his stutter worse than usual. Marguerite closed her face in that Norman way of hers and put another log on the fire. Gives her time to think.

The new one warmed her hands at the fire before she sat. No taller than Denis, which is not tall at all. Dyed hair, busty. I presumed the latter was an advantage far as Denis was concerned, but the way she went after him he may never even have had the time to notice.

All that was fine, allowing for Denis's past history of getting hurt and Marguerite's history of looking out for him. She never adopted or stood for him in any office or church, but he still called her Marraine, to the point that everyone who knew and loved her called her Godmother too. His own mother died an alcoholic slob—I never found out what drove it—in a shambles of a house above the village. He'd fallen out with most of his family. All either sharks or wife beaters, it was hard to see where Denis the meticulous housekeeper came in at all. The new busty one was fine too if you didn't know about the money Denis had stashed away from shift work in the car components factory over twenty-five years, and the odd jobs he did the rest of the time to keep himself from getting depressed. Gardening, chopping wood, anything requiring a strong arm. Gardens as meticulous as his house. You'd meet him at high speed anywhere in the region, some machine or other sitting in the bed of his truck.

So why was this busty American interested in our hard-working stuttering Denis? It seems she found him in his usual campsite over in Brittany, where all our ageing bachelors go each year to drink greater than usual quantities of whiskey and Coke, for some reason eschewing the local taste for Calvados. Their way of breaking free, maybe. Education or money can help you break free, but even they are not enough sometimes. These guys had neither.

'She smells of smoke,' I said to Marguerite on a turn in the kitchen to get drinks.

'It's the open fire over at Denis's,' said Marguerite.

'It's proximity to hell,' I said. 'She's so near hell you can see sparks.'

'Get out of my kitchen and go pretend you're a host,' said Marguerite.

'Your kitchen, your house, your country.'

'Your fault.'

'Every house needs a scapegoat.'

I knew she was smiling and waving a kitchen utensil at my back as I headed off with the drinks.

'Don't do that,' I said, 'I have eyes in the back of the head.'

Sitting in front of the hot stove I rememorize the stifling heat as they kettled us into the Falaise pocket that final summer, the welcome sounds of Polish and Canadian voices that meant it was over at last. I can still smell it, and hear the flies buzz. Women fed their children under muslin for months afterwards, so they wouldn't swallow the flies congregating on the dead—especially the horses—and the living.

The camp at Damigny to which the Americans delivered us was better than all that, no matter how much work the French made us do or how many of us died every day. Some of us were even DOA—the Allies handed over those they thought in the worst condition, then blamed the French for not looking after us. Some of the guys complained that we were paying the price, being punished, while those responsible got back to Germany or away to South America.

Getting out of that atmosphere—even to clear mines—was fine with me. I was teamed up with a Croat and a Pole. Escorted by an armed Frenchman day and night, we got clogs, better rations and lived among ourselves in pitch-roofed huts near a village. After clearing mines all day, the Croat played harmonica in the evening. Kids passed twice a day herding goats. We became almost human. In the camps further east, the thing was far from over, and the process of becoming human again hadn't even started. Our equipment was lousy, and men on the coastal dunes were getting blown up by the hour. The constant risk of death kept us from thinking about our homes and families. I'd had no replies to my letters for eighteen months.

Denis's new woman was called Diana. Huntress, definitely. She praised the escalopes, the way foreigners do, even before they've tasted the food. Things were going well enough until she started poking at our backgrounds. My new hand is always an excuse for this. You're sitting there feeding and watering someone and they start quizzing you. For sixty years researchers have been coming here asking war questions. Marguerite and I mostly manage to avoid them, and we never volunteer for interviews or films. The locals don't suggest us either because she and I, we're kind of off the scale— pariahs. Brits who buy houses here now have the decency never to mention the war. Most locals never talk about it, to officialdom or anyone else. We live from day to day, savoring each one for what it is. Marguerite and me and *Existentialism for Dummies*: freedom and choice and how to live your life. Oh, when drink is consumed I've heard the occasional outburst: about girls raped by soldiers, Allied bombings of the towns and cities, Germans coming to farms demanding food. Then they remember me and shut up.

And now here's this dyed-hair flibbertigibbet who wants to *know*.

'And who are *you*?' I asked, leaning over the table. 'We live here, you're visiting; tell us your story first.'

She looked surprised.

'A-a-a-a-lex...' Denis stuttered.

'Can I presume you're all finished with those plates,' said Marguerite, getting up and giving me her strictest eyeballing.

'Well, I teach English now,' Diana said obligingly. 'I was a masseuse back home.'

Her French pronunciation was awful. A *ma ssouss*, she made it sound.

'A ma ssouss,' I repeated. I looked at Denis. Denis looked awestricken. A masseuse. I had visions of semi-prostitution. He'd dragged some hopeless cases in for our approval, but this one knocked them all into a cocked hat.

'I'm from Washington State.'

She said something about three cities and a nuclear power facility that was the main employer. She was honest enough to admit that she was teaching English only because she could speak it.

'They don't ask for any other qualification. Butts on seats,' she said. 'The French get the real jobs and we fill the gaps. We don't get paid for holidays; we'll never get a pension. No one cares if anyone learns English anyway—it has to do with public money going around in circles. You can make a living at it,' she added, 'the problem is getting the right paperwork.'

She had come on some temporary exchange deal, but her time was soon up. She looked lovingly at Denis.

That's when the penny dropped. She needed papers. She was white, so the police wouldn't stop her in the street, but she needed papers to have the right to work.

'This is the world upside down,' I said, 'Americans coming to Europe to look for work.'

'I want to set up my own business,' she said. 'Herbs and spices. I can run it from home.'

I wondered where home would be. Marguerite gave me a black look that said: *Give it up, now.*

I gave it up. I have been following Marguerite's orders since the day I met her.

We walked into the farmyard, me and another POW—the Croat—a few paces behind someone from the Service des Prisonniers de Guerre. He'd explained that it was a big farm that was short of hands. We all knew it was short of hands because the hands had been taken away to Germany ages before, and only God knew where they were now. Like my mother and brothers. Like chocolate biscuits today, hands were shipped all over Europe, crisscrossing each other on roads and trains.

We walked up to the kitchen door and the man from the Service knocked. The person who opened the door was the tiniest adult I had ever seen, her smile elfish. This was Marguerite, barely out of her teens, working on farms since she was twelve. She had already acquired an authority she never lost since. She looked us up and down.

'So you're the boys who relaunched local industry,' she said.

The Service guy was so surprised he said nothing.

'They're busy day and night making clothes and beds for ye,' she went on.

She yelled for the boss.

When he came, he seemed disappointed in us. He was more than a little dubious about my hand. Although I'd kept it in my pocket, the man from the Service mentioned it. No doubt he didn't want to have to walk all the way back again with another prisoner. The farmer agreed to take us on trial.

Diana's new home turned out to be an old barn and two caravans on a hectare of land nearer the coast that she'd bought for a song. They alternated between Denis's place and hers. There was lots of talk about makeovers and the style she'd do it in—neither heavy-beamed Norman nor Zen, she said. She started dragging furniture home from antique dealers and second-hand stores, before they'd even made the structure sound.

Denis did fewer jobs for others and more for her. His machines sat unoiled and unused, and people phoned to complain that their lawns and bushes were growing wild. The huntress obviously made sure he kept his main job at the factory.

I passed her place a few times when I knew they weren't there. Diana had installed brand new and highly visible signs saying 'Lands Protected—Fur and Feather' and giving the address of some wildlife association. I wondered how Denis and his hunting buddies felt about this, but he seemed to have stopped hunting too. Diana dropped in occasionally to see Marguerite to get info on cooking or remedies, on some back-to-nature trip, her fingers dark from collecting fruit. Looking for alcohol to make sloe gin. The hair dye seemed to be growing out, something brighter underneath. I wondered how Denis was coping, but didn't dare ask. He wasn't my godchild, or even my pretend godchild, but that wasn't the problem. Marguerite isn't a great talker and her motto was if it isn't broke, don't fix it. I suppose we were happy that Denis was getting some loving. And hoping it wouldn't finish up like all his other affairs.

One day in spring I went by and found vans and scaffolding and a company getting ready to put a new roof on Diana's barn. Turned out she'd borrowed the money from Denis.

'Borrowed?'—I said to Marguerite later—'How's she going to pay it back with those skivvy wages of hers?'

When I asked Denis, he said, 'There will be nothing between us anyway, we've decided to get married.'

'Time must be running out on her,' I told Marguerite.

'Don't spoil it. We have to hope it works out for him,' she said. 'He won't get many more chances.'

'I don't see what I can do for him anyway,' I said, 'the dope's supposed to be grown up, and we're not even relatives.'

I did try. I caught him alone one day and suggested he do a pre-nup, a common enough thing in France. I thought it would be a test for her. He said it would be like accusing her of being after his money.

I said nothing. I have little enough myself, the house is in Marguerite's name, so I'm no example. My old grandfather, referring to another mindless war, used to say a man only needs six feet of land, enough to be buried in.

That will be plenty for me.

My diminished hand and arm proved to be as good as whole ones. The Croat and I set up quarters in the barn and worked from dawn till dusk, him and Marguerite explaining how to do most of the jobs I had never done before, me the boy from a modest family on his way to a university education. I learned about farming and carpentry. All I knew up to then was how to compare one philosopher with another, and a bit of French. After a few months, I was Mr Fixit. Whatever stuffing was left in me after Russia, Marguerite knocked it out and replaced it with good food in the back kitchen. We put on weight and got a tan.

Nine months later the man from the Service came back to explain that we could now sign up to be 'free workers,' which would entitle us to a month's holidays. The Croat and I signed up immediately. We would be replaced by others, either POWs or immigrants. No one referred to the fiction that we would come back or the fact that the journey on foot would take more than our holiday time, one way.

Marguerite helped us sew up two homemade rucksacks. She filled them with food for the journey. We set off in late spring, among the first of the former POWs to leave.

13

In early summer Diana and Denis decided to celebrate their engagement and marriage in one mad week. Diana installed a blue-and-white-striped marquee in the field behind the barn, and ordered up crates of drink. It was a raucous affair with all Denis's hunter friends, his odd-job friends, his drinking friends and a group of bikers he knew from camping. An odd group of her friends flew in from the U.S. west coast. These included an Indian chief and a sociologist, who was apparently a local politician and a defender of sex workers.

There was motorbike noise and fumes and music for days. Anyone who went by was treated to food and drink and many people did, just to see the circus. The immediate neighbors, the Langlois, threatened to go for the police. The police wouldn't have come, busy as they were elsewhere: teenagers were making two hundred Euros an hour from their bedrooms, selling webcam sex shows.

I read from *Ouest France*: 'Baby klappe hatches are being provided in Berlin as an alternative dropping point for mothers otherwise desperate enough to kill their babies in an apparent outbreak of infanticide—'

'Stop reading that stuff,' said Marguerite; 'you're tortured enough without it.'

When the fuss died down, Denis seemed curiously deflated. He visited us more often. He was supposed to be learning English. I got him to give us a sampling. From the little I knew, it seemed she was laughing at him.

By summer, a crack appeared.

'She refuses to go camping in Brittany,' he told us.

'Makes sense,' said Marguerite. 'Bunch of boys in a tent.'

'She wants to go down the coast,' he said.

'Certainly more chic,' I said.

There was something about visiting Pierre Loti's house, a writer Diana had studied at school.

So that was what they did.

'Must have been only scouting, the day she found him on the campsite,' I told Marguerite.

When we got to Nuremberg we split up. The Croat went south, I went on towards the north east.

(The next time I saw the Croat he had spent five years in the French Foreign Legion, had French nationality, worked in a northern coal mine and had a Polish wife—a tall young woman trying to climb out of an obese body. He sat and drank forever at a black-topped table, occasionally reaching out for cake, scooping it up by the handful, never looking right or left. I didn't stay long.)

When I eventually arrived to where my village, house, and family should have been, I could find nothing. I circled excitedly. By evening I collapsed in a ditch from exhaustion and confusion. The next day was no better. Hardly anyone passed, and those who did knew nothing. There was a blasted aspect to the landscape, and an irritating wind. I decided I'd lost my memory and wandered away.

Around mid-morning I came on a man sitting on a hummock, staring into space. He ignored me. I waited.

'Bodies everywhere,' he said, after a while. 'Bodies in dirty uniforms. Sweaty, suffering women in frocks. Smoldering houses invested by starving cats. Cold fabric of the priest's dirty habit, in from the cold with Extreme Unction. A boy with a bell and an incense-burner.'

He didn't seem to be talking to me.

I named my village, asked him how to find it. He ignored me. I decided he might be deaf.

'This is nothing, compared to those coming out of the camps. Men in rags too tired and scared to walk through an open gate. Red Cross. United Nations. Abjection.'

After a while, he turned, looked me up and down, then finally caught my eye.

'There's no point in looking, son,' he said gently. 'It's gone. And everyone in it.'

'Get away,' he said. 'Far as you can. They won't want you here. You will remind them of all that was bad and went wrong. They'll call you a Nazi.'

They occasionally called us that in France. Nevertheless, I turned on my heel and headed back the way I had come, the empty rucksack flapping at my back.

When Denis and Diana came back from the west coast, she was full of Pierre Loti and his house and his mad parties. Loti had once sent party invitations out a year in advance, so that everyone had enough time to learn medieval French, not to mention knocking together suitable costumes. He'd had two families, oriental lovers (male and female, it would appear), and had made his house into an oriental museum piece, with real sarcophagi in an Islamic-style prayer room. Diana was impressed by how ordinary the house appeared from the outside.

'Loti was ahead of his time,' I told Marguerite. 'They're all into stuff, these days. Stuff. A crisis is when they can't change their car annually.'

'I explained all that to you long ago,' she replied.

She'd once told me how the bigger landowners saw

themselves as a different race: *les possédants*, the ones who possess.

'The rest of us don't deserve a say in anything. They resent our having a vote, but it's good if we vote for them. They took over from the nobility after the Revolution.'

I'd seen them in action, the way they cliqued and dressed and looked down on people not like them.

'Used to call them bourgeois, the way I learned it.'

'Don't start with that capitalist guff again,' she sighed. 'If you wanted to be a communist you should've stayed over east.'

'Which is capitalist now anyway. Six feet, that's all I need.'

She sighed again loudly.

The journey back to France was harder, with no food, hardly any money and no family reunion to look forward to. Shoes worn and feet blistered, I went like the wind. I met, ate and got lifts with people fleeing in all directions. Everyone had a story that was sadder than the last. I watched sunrises and sunsets as if I'd never seen them before. I told myself that if I hadn't lost my reason up to now, I could hang onto it for another while. I remembered my grandfather's version of Nietzsche's motto 'What doesn't kill me makes me stronger:' 'What doesn't choke will fatten,' my father often said.

I even thought I was cured of emotion, but there was that small kernel of it that drew me back to Normandy—the only other place anyone had ever cared for me.

Another crack appeared in the works by Autumn. Mme Langlois—Diana's neighbor, the one she'd bought the barn from—accused Diana of witchcraft.

'Nothing new there,' said Marguerite.

It was a common accusation around here among the older women—the first word they went for when they felt things getting out of their control. What I liked about Marguerite was that she never got involved in this witchcraft talk, never accused anyone of it, even in anger. Some of the crones do it all the time, falling in and out of friendships with alarming regularity. Marguerite believes in Something or Someone Up Above, as she puts it, although she doesn't go to church. She even watches Mass on the telly on Sunday mornings, but if anyone comes in she switches it off.

'God has nothing to do with organized religion,' she said one day. 'I'm well placed to know about that.'

'Well, if there is a god, Up There or Down Here, he must be saving me for something,' I said, 'although at this stage I'm at a loss to see what I've been keeping my head below the parapet for, this long.'

'He's hoping you'll find meaning,' she said. 'Isn't that what you've been looking for, all these years? And he's saving you for me,' she said, stroking my cheek. 'For me.'

She grabbed her keys.

'Now let's visit Langlois and see what this is all about.'

I limped into the farmyard one sunny morning. Marguerite was watering what was still in the shade. She stood back from the flowers, the watering can outstretched in surprise.

'So even they didn't want you,' she said.

'I didn't find them,' I gasped.

Then I collapsed in tears.

She brought me to the barn and settled me in with bread and butter and milk. It was July 14th. Our replacements were off for the day and there was little to be done. She bathed my feet. She changed my clothes. She held me in her arms while I cried.

And while Churchill was making his speech in Metz about the rebirth of France, Marguerite and I made love. Or should I say, she made love to me, to stop me whimpering.

She told me she had divorced a husband who drank and beat her, and how the crones had ostracized her for it. One had even testified against her at the divorce proceedings.

'Women are supposed to stay put and take their medicine,' she said.

It was dark when we heard the others coming back from the fourteenth of July dance. Marguerite whispered, 'If you and I are to remain friends we mustn't do this again.'

Then she disappeared into the house.

What the current trouble seemed to be about was Diana the huntress throwing shapes at old Mr Langlois. This might be true or it might not. Marguerite and I had no love for either of the Langlois. Mme Langlois was one of these fervent Catholics who still respects what's left of the local nobility—the upper echelons of the possessors—and goes on outings organized by priests. Her car sports stickers touting right-wing Catholic groups. She and others would have had Marguerite's head shaved if our liaison had happened early enough for it. She couldn't stand me, although she had some spiel about good Germans, nice soldiers who were billeted in her house and used to throw her like a ball between them when she was a kid and her father was dying of hunger in a camp in the east. 'Komm, Catherine!' the soldiers would say to her. Langlois smiled as she told it, almost pleased with

19

herself. She wasn't just conflicted, I thought she was soft in the head. Although logic and reason are not the strongest points in western or any other culture, Langlois didn't seem to have even the minimum of these. *'Komm, Catherine…'* tended to ring in my head and Langlois as a child sometimes exercised my mind more than my own horrors.

Marguerite and I would've defended Diana anyway, because she was Denis's wife. The problem was that when we went over there to talk it over, Mme Langlois not only accused Diana of going after her husband. There was worse.

'She actually lowered her jeans and showed me her backside,' said Langlois.

'She *what?*' Marguerite blurted, smothering a giggle.

'Showed me her ass,' said the bigot. 'What she said, precisely, was "If you're interested in my ass, here it is."'

Take it easy, heart, I thought. *We've been through worse than bare asses.*

'Well, nobody died,' said Marguerite.

The bigot looked at her. If the evil eye had any power, Marguerite was a goner.

'Why would Diana do that?' Marguerite asked on the way home.

'America is like an elephant with an itch it can't scratch,' I said, mainly for something to say.

'I think you mean the American government,' said Marguerite.

She always says that. She said the same thing sixty years ago when we started going places together.

20

I bought an old motorbike and we would take off for the coast, Marguerite having forgotten her idea that we'd never remain friends if we made love again.

Marguerite had this thing about ocean liners, could never get enough of them. So I was jealous of ocean liners, especially American ones. We would spend Sundays in Le Havre, where most of the local boys were getting piecework for rebuilding the town, working as fast as they could. Many of the houses around here were paid and families reared on the rebuilding of towns like Caen, Le Havre and St Malo. I never even tried for such jobs, content to stay with Marguerite on farms. I thought no one would have wanted me anyway, although the French were shipping in cheap labor from all over: Germany, Poland, Italy, North Africa. I just kept a low profile and stayed where I was.

Diana started her own business, as planned, but not from home. Before anyone talked of a credit crunch she managed to squeeze county money and regional money and whatever was left of Denis's money. The thing was set up in a local industrial park and involved lots of packing equipment, plenty of high tech, someone to set up and run a website for mail order, and pharmaceutical standards of hygiene.

Even if she'd cleaned Denis out, we supposed that was okay as long as she stayed with him.

On the quay at Le Havre we stood, keeping our voices down, among American soldiers leaning against American cars, waiting and wanting to go home. Their uniforms weren't half so crisp or handsome as in the films that portrayed them. But they were better fed than us, from better-fed parents. Good teeth filled their big smiles. They smiled and waited and watched. Marguerite would watch the ships and I would watch her, in a yellow button-down dress with oranges and apples on it, watching those gigantic ships come and go, bearing glamorous passengers and other people's dreams. Her favorite liner was the Ile de France. Back in the village she would throw her hands together like a child and describe it to friends. One Christmas I found her a poster for the Cunard line. She installed it on the wall of our first house together. By then it was the '60s: the crones were being silenced by new clothes, new music, new mœurs. They didn't like us, but they had no power over us.

In autumn, I watch her again. Marguerite sits at the center of the big table in the local hall. It is so wide they have to shout across at us and make sign language. She shrugs. She is concentrating on the occasion, the ceremony, her job as hostess. It is her ninetieth birthday and she has been working on the menu for weeks with the caterer. She eats very little, picking and watching her guests. She supervises each serving, waits for reactions and comments, smiles when they come, sensitive to any praise or slight. When the main course is served, she does a tour of the table, chatting with each one, leaning on her stick.

Not eating, not settled, not at ease, just like her job on the farms, hovering near a table of eaters, wanting everyone to be fed and happy, barely as high standing as they are sitting. I watch her and wonder why she inflicts this on herself now, why she does it, and I tell myself—yet again—that she does it for the giving, of course, as she gave and gives to me and to all the others like Denis, other people's children, all her life. For the giving she never got herself. Marguerite first gave herself to me in the way she did everything else: it was her decision, not mine, it was her body and she had decided it.

22

On her first farm, at twelve years of age, they gave her bread and coffee three times a day, standing up in the kitchen with a farm boy. One day she started to vomit. When they finally consulted a doctor, he said she was malnourished. She was bedridden for weeks. After that, someone found her a good farm, where they tried to feed her up, coaxing her to eat.

'Much as I'd have liked, I couldn't oblige them.'

From then on she could no longer eat a proper meal, her stomach had shrunk. She enjoyed soup.

'Like an ailing beast, I didn't thrive. I stayed small and thin. It was like an insult to their goodness.'

She couldn't have children or at least none had appeared and no precautions were taken.

'Better that way,' she smiled that elfish smile. 'The bigots would go mad. Maybe the witches organized it.'

When I persuaded her to check with a doctor, he discovered a tumor.

'Take it all out, so,' Marguerite told him. 'That'll knock the laugh out of us.'

The doctor pretended to be shocked. French women didn't say that kind of thing, to doctors or anyone else.

Marguerite said the French ideal of a woman was Coco Chanel, and did everything she could to counter it. She also said some Frenchwomen didn't deserve the vote, even in 1945.

Sometime later it was my turn again, with another shrapnel flare-up.

'Shrapnel moves in strange ways,' said the surgeon, a plump man from Morocco. Marguerite refers to him as Le Gros—the Fat One.

Fancies himself as a wit.

'Pity it has no market value,' he said, 'we'd have made a fortune out of you.'

There was some kafuffle after Marguerite's birthday party. It started among the gauntlet of smokers outside the door. Diana wanted to go on someplace, Denis wanted to go home. She was all decked out in some glittery thing more suitable to New Year's. He was tired and had to get up in a few hours.

'The c-c-c-c-crisis is b-b-biting,' he said, 'this is no time to t-t-t-t-test the b-b-boss.'

He was right. Factories were closing left, right and center. Some of those that stayed open were on up to ninety days forced closure.

Diana finally went off with some of the others, while Denis went home.

Denis's original nosedive was due to some tart he'd picked up locally. She showed herself around with him then did a bunk with someone else. Denis spent months in bed, unable to get up. The second time he actually tried to kill himself with tablets, but Marguerite found him in time and nursed him back to health on her sofa. She even said we should import an Asian woman who'd be more sensitive to his needs and more appreciative of what she was getting.

'With his kind of luck,' I said, 'he'd get a dud.'

The herbs and spices business started well enough, but by the end of the year it too started to get hit by the economic crisis. The Euro was too high, Americans wouldn't buy. Sterling had slipped to the value of the Euro, so the Brits weren't buying either. This whole economic thing was going faster than the weather metaphors they gave it: tsunami, whatever.

The real estate market had already begun to flinch when Diana sold the barn to an English couple. They were either the last of the big spenders or they were oblivious to what was going on. Younger than our usual Brits, they kept coming to Marguerite with flowers and cakes. I kept wondering what they wanted from her.

'Maybe they want nothing,' Marguerite said. 'Some people want nothing, like your good self.'

Turned out they were looking for work.

'Now the world is really upside down,' I said.

Worse was to come. Diana had never really moved most of her personal belongings—what she referred to as her stuff—over to Denis's place.

One day in January I strolled by to find a removals truck outside the barn door. There was no sign of Diana. I stopped and asked the guys what was happening.

'Stuff is going to the States,' they said. 'Sale goes through tomorrow. We're getting extra pay for being double quick about it.'

Stuff was always a first priority, I thought.

We never saw her again. Diana had skipped with the barn money—her money, since she'd bought it before they married. Denis arrived the next day, pale, tearful and inarticulate. He first thought something had happened to her. He had searched high and low after work, not slept, not worked. Finally he went to the police. It was the police who told him she was leaving the country—they knew because of something to do with paperwork for the removals. He refused to stay and eat.

It snowed the next day, Saturday.

'Let's get Denis over for lunch,' said Marguerite. 'Cheer him up.'

He didn't pick up the phone, of course. Of course I went over there. A light dusting of snow had fallen. There were no footprints in his yard. Of course the door wasn't locked, and of course he was hanging from the rafters in an otherwise impeccably clean house.

I didn't have to tell Marguerite. She knew it from my step in the yard, then the look on my face. She put her hand to her chest.

She called the police and the funeral parlor and made all the arrangements.

A man came out with a catalogue you'd find funny if it wasn't sinister. Marguerite took advantage of the situation to make arrangements for us as well.

'Six feet,' I said.

Marguerite ignored me. 'No plastic crosses on the coffins,' she told him. Then, as if she knew something I didn't, 'Any of them.'

Organized religion wasn't going to have the last word.

She put her hand to her chest again.

A lawyer phoned looking for Denis. When Marguerite questioned him, he said that Diana had left massive debts related to her business. Because they had no marriage contract, Denis was responsible for debts incurred after the marriage.

'Well there's one thing he did well to duck out of,' said Marguerite. Then she bit her lip and wondered if he'd known this before he killed himself.

'It wouldn't have been a barrel of laughs for him,' I agreed. Then she told me to call the doctor.

I buried them both the same icy day. You can't fit two coffins in a hearse (not many people know that) so the cortege looked like something from a film, or an accident.

'Look after that handsome head of yours,' was the last thing she said to me. This is what I loved her for: pure disinterested caring for others. There was no side to Marguerite.

As the man from the funeral parlor drove me home, freezing fog hung low over the cathedral spire in Rouen. Highest spire in France, reaching after Somebody Up There. Unless He was now Somewhere Else, in a world upside down.

As we slowed in traffic crossing the bridge, I found myself a yard away from an elderly oriental on foot. He was wearing one of those old blue costumes the Chinese used to wear.

He caught my eye. Maybe the funeral car got his attention. His look was kindly. It said: *We've been through some things, you and me. We should have died several times. Better people than us did.*

Righteous Indignation

Mme F—Fernande to her friends—lives just around the corner from the canal bridge where Arletty pronounced the famous question: '*Atmosphère?*' with all that heavy Parisian irony. The Hotel du Nord, backdrop and title of the film, is still there, the canal and surroundings still one of the cool places to be, in Paris, in the summer.

At eighty-seven, Fernande well remembers the film, having been a bit of a goer herself, once. Although the younger crowd tend to find the Canal very *branché*, and are willing to pay higher prices to live on or near it, Fernande invariably turns her back on it, preferring to reach back toward the streets where she used to work as a *concierge*. She eats lunch every day in one of the cheap places along rue St Maur, has shandies with anyone who'll cooperate, and she's always willing to pay. She is well known to the new Arab and Berber owners of the rundown cafes with rotting awnings and poster photos of hillsides in Kabylie. Shandies remind her of the good times, when Georges was alive.

Fernande has two minders, although she'd rather have none, and there is some doubt as to whether she really needs any of them or if they actually need her more. One of them is a plump Portuguese with a pathological fear of old women being swindled, who watches over Fernande like a hawk. The Portuguese reports to the other minder, a cousin of Fernande, who is after the inheritance, and has every interest in keeping it intact.

Fernande dresses in vivid colors, flowered dresses with matching cardigans, shoes and jackets. Her former neighbor, Zorica, says she used to be very chic indeed, although now she looks slightly disheveled and has a tendency to slouch, moving in and out of the conversation and giving the minders an excuse to pretend she's lost the run of herself. She loves food and drink and if there are *amuse-gueules* on the table she digs into them absentmindedly before anyone else or before the drinks are served, suggesting that she is not quite with it. Another thing that annoys the minders is when she manages to give them the slip, which is as often as possible. It is quite a feat for her to make it all the way down the stairs where she lives, then hobble along the ill-mended streets and make her way up another set of stairs—this is not a neighborhood with many lifts, or even the space to install them, if money were to be found for the purpose—where she almost collapses after the effort and excitement of her escape. She often takes refuge with Zorica, where they chat and watch soaps for hours, talking intermittently, misunderstanding each other frequently. Fernande is on the ball for most things, yet can forget long-time neighbors or acquaintances in the house. Zorica, a foreigner and illiterate to boot, for whom Fernande read letters and interpreted bills over the years, merely shakes her head: Fernande can do no wrong. Zorica perceives her like a mother, and has missed her desperately since she left to look after her sister in a brand new apartment down the street: new building, public housing. Now that the sister has died, Mme F, as well as feeling lonely, is hoping City Hall will give her the rubber stamp to stay, but of course city

29

hall officials are saying, 'Why don't you go back to your own apartment?' Mme F likes it in the new building, where she has a view of the early seventeenth-century Hôpital St Louis, and in the distance Montmartre and the Sacré Cœur. Although it's a bit lonely, she manipulates the neighbors to do the shopping for her. The only shopping she does herself now is for *amuse-gueules*, in the Chinese or Arab late-night groceries. The minders are terrified she'll be mugged.

Yet Mme F can take care of herself. When the ground floor garage owner complains that she watered him as well as her geraniums, she silences him: 'And we're supposed to breathe exhaust fumes and say nothing, I suppose?' She is especially vigilant for car horn abuse, and rushed out recently to shake her fist at two motorbike policemen—who had the temerity to tootle their sirens gently once or twice behind a vehicle momentarily abandoned in the middle of the street. 'Do you want to deafen us or what?' she roared. '*Oh, ça va, ça va*,' the policemen replied patiently.

The Portuguese minder tells stories to anyone who'll listen, about other old ladies she's known who were had by crooks before leaving this world. Although she prefaces the stories with a 'Look at me, I'm hardly a likely candidate to be racist,' her stories are always just that. One old lady almost signed to purchase land and build a holiday complex on the Moroccan coast, she says, proposed to her by the Moroccan doctor treating her in the hospital. 'Found it in a drawer after she died,' says the minder. 'He's left now and gone home, so I can talk about it.' Listening to the Portuguese, one would be forgiven for thinking the whole quarter was full of rich elderly ladies and foreign crooks. Another woman, the Portuguese relates with relish, was pulling six hundred euros a week from a bank account and handing it over to someone who did her weekly shopping. 'She was black,' the Portuguese says loudly, glaring balefully down the street.

The Portuguese may be a bit paranoid, but she is an excellent watchdog for Mme F's cousin. One thing is sure: old Fernande might be losing her marbles, but her absentmindedness exists in direct proportion to the person with whom she is dealing. She has neighbors she likes, and has given them many of her belongings. The Portuguese, however, is convinced that the neighbors, a youngish couple, are robbing Mme F, slowly but surely. She has been to their apartment, she says, and seen the stuff there. The Portuguese and the inheriting cousin have warned Fernande, over and over, NEVER to open the door to ANYONE. Fernande shrugs and says, 'No pockets in a shroud.' She hopes to rid herself of most of her belongings before she passes on, and cares not a whit for the inheriting cousin or the Portuguese. 'They are a pain,' she says. When she really needs help they are never too pleased to be asked, so the hell with them. Fernande tends to get very annoyed about the non-cooperation of her poor old feet and legs, and often has to be assisted home after one of her shandy escapades. The minders say she should use the walking stick they got her.

One of her excuses for frequent escape is the two apartments in her former building. One of these, on the third floor, she owns, but had to abandon it and rent one on a lower floor when the stairs became too much. When she wants to collect her mail, Fernande makes her way up there on her own, and if Zorica isn't there and she can't manage to open her door, she stands on the stairs yelling 'Anyone home?' in a pathetic voice that is full of power, until someone shows up. Invariably she has the wrong key, or the overhead light bulb has blown, and the concierge has to be called out. It is often the concierge's husband who arrives, a cigarette to the side of his mouth, bearing a ladder and a new bulb, giving Fernande a side look across his pencil moustache. He knows Fernande was once the concierge. Perhaps he wonders if he and his wife will finish up like her if they don't beat a retreat to Portugal before falling apart. Then he wrestles Fernande's three sets of keys from her, opens the door, deposits her inside, and leaves Zorica or one of the others to decide what to do with her.

Both of Mme F's apartments are monuments to a kind of kitsch which Susan Sontag never dreamed of. Fernande calls it untidiness, and only apologizes for it vaguely, as for a crime perpetrated by someone else. The rented apartment is the most kitsch of the two, as if Mme F had made up for Georges' absence, and her descent to the first floor, by a flurry of foreign holidays and purchases. Glass-fronted cupboards overflow with dolls of every shape and size, from every ethnic grouping. Dolls from some demented *Carmen* dance across chests of drawers and, like Zorica's flowers, look as if they are about to make a getaway across the ceiling and walls and back to some eternal rave or other. A check has to be done upstairs as well, in the smaller room she and Georges shared for some sixty years, as the door seems loose and everyone is worried about possible squatters.

In the upstairs apartment, squatters would be comfortable if in a sort of time warp. The kitsch here is slightly less frenetic, with reminders and black-and-white photos of her and him all over the place. Lace doilies cover a small early-model TV set and radio. A well-worn carpet occupies the middle space. Old post office calendars block up missing window-panes. A wall-bed clad in Formica looms large on one side of the room. Fernande turns on her heel with an agitated sigh and walks back down, having wiped all memory of this life from her mind. Let the cousin have it when she dies. The room, for her, died with Georges.

She is much more intrigued by the notice of a registered letter she has received from the concierge, and is adamant that she wants to go to the post office and get it, in spite of warnings of standing in a queue and needing an ID. Clasping the notice to her front, she sets off for the post office on Zorica's arm, with a determined air.

Out on the street it is hot. There is a hum of sewing machines in the air. Bags of offcuts from the morning's work have already been left out for the bin collection. Mme F tells Zorica that city hall has invited her to the old folks' annual dinner in a local restaurant. 'Used to invite us once a month,' she adds, 'before the Right got in. Now the Left are back, it doesn't look like they'll go back on it.' It doesn't occur to her that Zorica, past the age of retirement but a foreigner and therefore a non-voter, is invited nowhere. Mme F makes jokes about voting for the National Front in the European elections, and there is no guarantee she wouldn't do so. Yet she isn't racist. Several young men sit on a doorstep and study the two old ladies with interest. One, of North African origin, is looking for a row. When Mme F refuses to mount the high footpath near him—because she avoids high steps of any kind—he asks aggressively, 'Afraid to walk right by an Arab, are you?' 'Didn't know you were an Arab, did I,' retorts the bold Mme F, quick as a flash. He doesn't quite know what to say to that.

Zorica too is no stranger to righteous indignation, although she has never been able to develop it sufficiently. The finest example she has never forgotten is the day, shortly after her arrival, when—having learned what it was and how to ask for it—she ventured into a bakery shortly before midday and asked for a croissant. The bakery assistant glowered, consulted her watch and bellowed at the now deeply embarrassed Zorica: 'The idea!' and looking to the other customers for confirmation of the misdeed. Trying to buy a croissant near midday! Parisians made the laws, and would make sure everyone else followed them. If not, they might erupt in violence again as they had done in 1789. The threat was there. It was effective. French farmers frequently made use of a similar threat, by throwing vegetables and fruit around the motorways, or dumping animal carcasses in front of a local *Mairie*. In Paris, the threat had reached its finest expression in righteous indignation, and required no further action.

They are in luck—at the post office there's no queue and Mme F actually has her ID card with her. They limp over to the desk. 'This looks like *Monsieur* F,' says the official behind the counter, examining the envelope. 'Couldn't be, he died three years ago,' says Mme F. 'Let's see the letter anyway,' says Zorica. The clerk returns with a letter from the electricity company addressed to Monsieur Georges F, which he says he cannot give to Mme F because it is not addressed to her.

'But Georges died three years ago and I've been paying the bills ever since,' wails Mme F. The man behind the counter studies her briefly, but he has no intention of giving in: 'Have to produce a death certificate,' he says. Mme F doesn't bat an eyelid. Drawing herself up to her full, unrheumatic height, she makes an announcement, to all and sundry, at the top of her voice: '*Elle est belle, la France*.' Then she and Zorica limp defiantly out for the long walk home. Zorica has to refuse her offer of drinks at every corner bar.

The minders take care of the registered letter—which was about nothing important, in fact. Mme F is admonished again about unaccompanied journeys abroad. The next time Fernande turns up *chez* Zorica she is considerably disheveled, but defiantly wearing crumpled mauve from head to foot. She leans on the new walking stick. There's a nephew she likes to whom she'd like to leave the room when she dies, but it would cost him huge state taxes since he's only a distant relative. Maybe she'll just sell it now and give him the money, thereby avoiding inheritance taxes. She'll think about it. Let the minders go to hell, she says. She never carries more than twenty Euros in her purse, so there's no point in anyone trying to rob her. And they're hardly likely to want to rape her, now. She and Zorica have iced tea from the painted bottle, cooled by plastic colored golf balls from Zorica's freezer. There's no shortage of *atmosphère*.

OLD WOOD BEST TO BURN

1965

Angel walked northwards—away from his own country, Spain—for the second time in five years, a free man after five years in the French Foreign Legion, a new French passport in his pocket. He kept going for days on end, got lifts on trucks, slept in barns, ate with people working in the fields. He wasn't sure what he wanted, but he didn't want to go home.

At St Gervais du Bosc, something made him stop. It could have been the familiar location: *garrigue* above, vineyards and orchards below, the village crouched at the butt of the hill where the water was available. He entered the café, stood at the bar and ordered a beer.

'*Trabajo?*' he asked the cafetier when the beer was almost finished. His mix of French and Spanish didn't faze people in the Languedoc, their own language poised somewhere between the two.

'You missed the grape harvest,' the cafetier said. Angel knew that. Agricultural work was the only thing he knew besides fighting Arabs.

'Boismal could use someone who can prune vines,' another client offered. 'The last man hung himself from a beam in the kitchen.'

At the upper end of the village stood a big old house on three floors, one above the hill, one below, and one level with the road. A little apart from the other houses, its irregular angles were resisting but nevertheless undergoing severe renovation.

Angel stood at the door and shouted '*Maison?*' a few times until a disgruntled elderly woman shuffled out in slippers. This was Boismal's wife. She put him in a sitting-room. Angel realized it was the first real house—with women—that he'd been in for eight years, if you didn't count the whorehouse in Algiers.

Warts and blotches covered Boismal's skin. He had a hacking cough. This didn't stop him being master of the moment. He pronounced the name the French way. *Ann-jell.*

'I'll take you,' he announced benevolently, 'lowest hourly rate. Under the table. I'll deduct a small rent for a house in the village. Start pre-pruning tomorrow.'

Number 6, rue Sans Nom was a three-story house with one room on each floor. The ground floor cellar had a bulging outside wall and contained a toilet. A steep staircase led to a room with a sink.

'Kitchen,' Boismal said, as if it were true. A tall dresser kept some of the ceiling from falling in. 'Hard winter snow lay around attics till it melted,' Boismal shrugged. 'Bit of a clean-up and it'll be fine.'

At the top was an attic bedroom containing a rabbit hutch. Someone had dipped a sponge in deep blue wash and stippled the white walls. Layers of dust covered the forgotten bunches of dried onions that hung neatly from a shelf, and equally forgotten bunches of grapes that hung from big hooks.

Back in the kitchen, alone, Angel didn't wonder which

hook his predecessor had used.

A thorough cleaning of new premises with little or no equipment was something Angel had learned in the Legion. He made a broom from twigs and cord and went to work. Rue Sans Nom, a street in existence since medieval times, was narrow and dark. The vaulted cellar bore traces of *verdigris* which the women had once carried to the market, on foot, twenty-five kms away. The musty smell reminded Angel of the cellar at home where a few goats were kept. As he scrubbed and dusted, he thought of his journey from home to here.

1957

Home was a small village near Valencia. Angel hadn't been very good at school, but he liked his old teacher, especially on wet days in winter. '*Valentia* in Latin means 'strength,' 'valor'' the old man told his unruly pupils. 'Then the Berbers came and called it *Balansiyya*.' He drew out the word and the boys giggled at his pronunciation. 'Listen well,' the old man insisted. 'Information and ideas will help while away your time in the fields. Some Roman historians were farmers too.'

Angel's older brother Rodrigo suddenly appeared before the glass window at the top of the classroom door.

'Sir!' he burst in, 'Oh, sir! Please can I have my brother— the floods have carried people away!'

Their parents were never found. Angel left school and he and his brother worked so hard on the little farm that Rodrigo forgot that he bore the same name as El Cid, until his childhood sweetheart, Gloria, reminded him.

Before leaving for military service Angel, a skinny teenager

38

who didn't even curse, went to see his old schoolmaster one last time. It was winter. He listened outside the classroom door as the master talked about a French monk who had once been bishop of Valencia. 'For centuries, government of our region seesawed between Spaniards and Moors.' The boys were quiet, glad to be indoors and resting. 'Later it was besieged by the English, and even the French. A peasant carries the blood of all cultures, working the land in spite of all the wars carried on around him.'

The boys stirred and Angel knew the master had risen from his desk. 'Never forget,' the old man shouted above the noise.

Later, on the train with his fellow conscripts, laughing and joking to hide their fear, Angel didn't look back or wonder when he would see again the lagoons, the rice fields, the oranges bright in the trees and the *garrigue* behind. He didn't understand the proverb his master had imparted before he left: '*Quemad viejos leños, leed viejos libros, bebed viejos vinos, tened viejos amigos.*'

1965

After a sound first night's sleep in 6, rue Sans Nom, Angel rose at sunrise and went to meet Boismal's old vines. Among these lines of tortured old friends, he clipped and trimmed and hummed, feeling the familiar strain on his back. At ten a.m. he ate olives and bread and drank half a bottle of the local *piquette* from the village shop. Around two he went home, made a tortilla and salad and had a snooze. Later, back in the vineyard, he watched the gnarled little shadows lengthen. Above the village, the dark *garrigue* was still in blazing sunlight, but the valley floor was already dark. The *bosc*, after which the village had been named, had burnt one summer, leaving one side of the mountain looking like an elephant's hide. Angel could still distinguish the old hill terraces, each with its little grove of olive trees, many of which were now being re-invaded by surrounding bush. Walls that once contained the terraces, if not tended, would one day crumble. For Angel forthcoming disaster meant two things: one, that he himself was not in trouble even if someone else was, and two, that there'd be work to do in the future, which made him feel secure. As smoke rose languorously from his home-made brazier—a rusty barrel split in two and mounted on wheels—it seemed to him that St Gervais might be okay. He made bundles of clippings for barbecuing chops and sausage and maybe even the odd fish.

1958

After training, he and his fellow-conscripts found themselves in Ifni in the Western Sahara. 'You are holding Spanish Southern Morocco against bands of guerrillas coming in from Mauritania and Algeria,' the sergeant said. None of them cared about Saharawi politics, or deals between France and Spain. The sergeant handed them a Spanish communiqué stating 'You are protecting the zone from those who disobeyed the king of Morocco.'

They knew nothing of the wiliness of the new Moroccan king. They disliked the food and the nights were cold. The new uniform chafed Angel's skin. Comrades were being killed by groups of guerrillas in repeated bouts of fierce fighting. 'You will be part of Operation Ouragan,' the sergeant said, 'a

Franco-Spanish effort. You'll back up paratroopers dropped into Smara.'

1968

Because Angel was accustomed to adapting to new circumstances, Boismal quickly saw that he knew his job and employed him officially, for full time work but at low wages. Angel came and went, becoming acquainted with Marinette and her stories of the past, as well as Simone and her preoccupations with the present, and enjoying René Boismal Jr's visions for a shining future with a revamped Coopérative.

'They're mixing good and bad grapes and making slop,' René would say. 'Now that heavy Algerian wine is finished they'll have nothing to mix the slop with. I'll plant new vines, get some quality going. Mark my words, the old man'll have to give in.'

They'd raise a glass. René would say what a loss Algeria was, although he didn't really care because he wanted change. Everyone wanted something. Thinking about such things made Angel's head spin.

When a hot wind blew sand from the south under the door in rue Sans Nom, Angel recalled the sandstorms of that early spring as the Spaniards and French swept through the Rio de Oro together, gaining courage as they went. 'Valor and strength!' Angel and the others cried. Few of them were killed. When it all became routine, Angel's dark beard grew faster and he spat and cursed like the older men, although he still didn't feel quite like the others. Now it seemed that all of his life had been spent trotting behind everyone else, trying to fit in.

A neighbor rented Angel a small garden next to the irrigation canal. He grew tomatoes and peppers, carrots, turnips, green beans and soggy potatoes for tortillas, his favorite lunch which he usually prepared the night before and ate cold, out among his friends, the vines. His relentless routine betrayed no visible difference between himself and his neighbors or the other men in St Gervais. But apart from René Boismal—his only real acquaintance—the local men kept their distance. The very real difference was that Angel was the only man without land of his own or even the promise of it. Angel was aware of this, but gave the matter as little consideration as he had other such aspects of his life, for what could he do about it? He sent money home to Rodrigo regularly. Rodrigo wrote very occasionally. 'My hands shake from work,' he wrote unsteadily. 'We're building a two-room place by the sea for renting to tourists.'

The news from Spain was confirmed in the autumn by the Spaniards who arrived for grape-picking.

Boismal Jr had known them since he was a kid.

'The Rubios have been coming for generations. This year one of the boys has brought his new wife.' Boismal laughed. 'They work so fast they outpace the lady of the house, *La Meneuse*; not the done thing at all.'

Angel often sat with the Rubios on the village square, watching the last of the tourists eat out, aware that this would set him further apart from the villagers.

'France is very expensive, compared to Andalusia,' they told him.

The new Rubio wife did all their cooking from food they'd brought with them, in the small bare house that was their free lodgings. Angel often heard a pressure cooker as he walked by and guessed chickpeas.

'Near Algeciras,' they replied, brightening, when he asked where they were from.

'You'd have passed Valencia on your way up,' Angel said.

They smiled. The Spaniards and Angel nodded to three boys Angel had seen around the village.

'From Morocco, Cameroon and Northern Ireland,' the Rubios told him. 'All students, they argue all day among the vines then hitch a ride into town in the evenings to drink and meet girls.'

'That is just the beginning,' the oldest Rubio woman said. 'Machines will soon take the place of all of us.'

1960

The day the army had let them go, the first thing Angel did was phone his brother Rodrigo. The grocery store, in the same street as Rodrigo's house, had always been everyone's telephone exchange and message center. The grocer replied, sent a child with the message, and told Angel to phone back in a while.

By the time Rodrigo finally came to the phone, Angel was almost out of change and Rodrigo was out of breath.

'I was working.' He sounded rattled.

'Well, I'm through here, I could come home and help.'

'I can manage the farm,' Rodrigo replied brusquely. The real problem seemed to be that the farm was too small to bring in enough to rear a family. 'We're married now,' he said, 'me and Gloria.'

Then Rodrigo's tone changed. 'Apartments on the coast

for tourists are the coming thing.'

Angel waited for more then realized that was all he was going to get. After waiting for a while, Rodrigo finally said what was on his mind: could Angel keep sending the money?

Angel left the phone booth and walked for a long time without purpose. In a café in Perpignan, a family—their accents markedly different from those of the locals—described, in a mix of Spanish, French and Arabic, how it was, 'down there' and wondered what they were to do now, in this France which was foreign to them.

'We have French papers but we never set foot in the place before,' they appealed. 'Not even our fathers ever visited.'

'Maybe France hasn't time, place or money for *pieds noirs.*' A man at the bar winked at Angel. 'Ye got the best of Algeria, but now that ye're refugees, don't expect the best of here as well.'

The *pied noir* father ordered his wife and family out. '*Fissa!*' he hissed in the Maghrebi dialect learned by his parents and grandparents.

Angel got up too and headed straight to the recruitment center of the French Foreign Legion. After passing the tough initial physicals and medicals, he only just passed the IQ test. Most of his fellow aspirants were dismissed. After that there were four months of even harder training, walking and running, day and night, carrying heavy packs often containing just sand. The trip in the truck to Marseilles, although hot and uncomfortable, provided a panorama of a hot dry landscape that was familiar.

In no time at all Angel found himself back in North Africa, working in the mess kitchens. This time it was Algeria and once again the enemy North Africans. His colleagues called the locals 'Arabs,' but more often '*melons*.' '*Tuer les melons—dadadadada!*' the legionnaires would imitate the sound of gunfire, and laugh.

1980s

By the early 1980s René Boismal Jr was married and refereeing arguments between his wife and mother over the color of curtains at home. Sometimes, when René talked of '*ma vieille*,' my old lady, Angel wasn't sure which woman he was referring to.

Increasingly, Angel took supper in the local restaurant, his only luxury. He smiled to himself as he handled the knife and fork delicately, relishing fancy desserts like *crème brulée* or the sweet crêpes they brought *flambée*'d to his table. That invariably got attention. He always slyly eyed the other diners under the stone vaults.

It was here one evening that Angel's fancy desserts drew him into talk with an English couple, he of tall military bearing, she equally lanky with a wide-brimmed straw hat and a noisy come-hither attitude. Angel was pleased because they spoke to him, and they liked him because they could understand the peculiar French he spoke.

On the husband's retirement from a multinational, they had bought a huge old house with vineyards and olive groves in an isolated spot above the village at the back of the *cirque* formed by the river. Now they lived here permanently and were struggling with everything: climate, farming, house. Very soon all three were watching out for each other in the evenings, having a carafe of rosé or sweet crêpes at adjacent tables, or together if there wasn't much room. Conscious that they were different, Angel was very careful not to encroach on their time or space. When they used the familiar '*tu*' he stuck to a respectful '*vous*.'

One evening the couple arrived at the restaurant to find it packed with tourists, a poetry reading in full swing. Angel sat in the middle, odd-man-out in his working clothes and three-day beard. They strained their necks for spare seats and caught his eye. He squeezed them in beside him and yelled for food. He was a little drunk. He was fighting with old Boismal about wages and conditions. He was going to see some sort of tribunal tomorrow and was very nervous: 'My balls are in a cravat,' he said. Boismal's terms were just not good enough. Boismal was ill, and crabby, saying take it or leave it. Angel was threatening to take it a lot further. It seemed Angel had decided, for the first time, which side he was on.

'Come over tomorrow evening after the tribunal and I'll cook you dinner,' the Englishwoman said to Angel.

Her husband nodded.

For a moment Angel looked puzzled, even shy. Then he raised his glass and said loudly, '*Viva la Revolución!*' They drank to that, finished the bottle and ordered another.

1960

Angel's first drinking bouts were among argumentative legionnaires. This involved political discussion—even they understood that de Gaulle's offer of self-determination to the Algerians had outraged the local French population. 'Serious trouble brewing—French against French,' the sergeant warned. 'Don't get rat-assed tonight.' Newspapers were full of the posturing of generals and statesmen. Rumors and counter-rumors bounced around them of possible army revolt and military take-overs. 'Tomorrow we leave the desert for Algiers to back up 1st REP paratroopers.'

In Algiers, the legionnaires remained apart from the French row, trained dogs waiting for the order to strike. On those clear cool days, amidst the rattle of trolley-buses and the tapping of glaziers repairing shattered windows, Angel noticed chic French girls and beautiful dark girls. In spite of the tension, many of them eyed the smart young men in their smart white hats. Even wearing his *képi*, Angel was far too shy to even think of speaking to them.

One evening, carried away by the evening street sounds, by drink, by his companions, he was led to a whorehouse, where the women were subject to checks by Legion doctors.

Angel's young woman had the unaccustomed features of a South American.

'*Hola,*' she said.

The business between them was dismal. As she buttoned him up again like his mother used to, Angel's attention was drawn to a reproduction above her bed. He didn't understand why the girl in the foreground lay stiff and nakedly white against the deep blue, green and red background.

'What is wrong with her?' he asked.

'Paul Gauguin, *Loss of Virginity,*' the girl said, matter of factly.

'Is that meant to be a fox at her shoulder?' Angel asked.

The girl nodded. 'Where I come from, it is the animal of the devil.'

Angel looked alarmed.

'Don't worry,' she said, 'you're no fox. Anyway, the real devil was Gauguin—he got the model pregnant then walked away.'

Angel had never had such a conversation before, least of all with a woman. Afterwards in the barracks, he found he couldn't lie like the others, and said nothing.

'Angel's in love!' they laughed.

1980s

After the tribunal determined the conditions of his job with Boismal (minimum wage, regular hours, written arrangements for the rent of rue Sans Nom), he headed off for the *Mas du Cirque*, still suffering from a hangover. Two cars were parked in the avenue. Three German shepherds bounded out the gate and Angel was impressed when the biggest took his wrist in its teeth and led him straight to its master.

The English couple gave him whiskey—'Hair of the dog,' they said—and took him on a tour of the property. The stone walls had been tastefully pointed. There were bright new shutters in pale green. Inside flagged floors, old furniture, patchwork quilts, Persian carpets and books abounded. A superb fitted kitchen opened onto a terrace with a gigantic pool. Angel had never seen so much vegetation used purely for decoration.

Then suddenly through another door it all came to a halt in a series of derelict rooms with a patchwork of cracked terracotta, open fireplaces, old wallpaper, dust. There were ladders, signs of work begun.

'Our son,' the Englishman said. 'Had to go back to college. Be back next year to carry on.'

'Now—I bet you're hungry,' she said.

They dined outdoors. Angel was astonished to find that good cuisine other than Mediterranean existed. There was still enough light to distinguish the *cirque* floor, once the village wheat field, now a balding football ground. Olive and fruit trees had been left to their devices for decades.

'Those olive trees are sick,' said Angel.

'Bug of some kind,' the Englishman said.

'I might have a cure for that,' said Angel.

'Why don't you come up and have a look at them,' she asked. 'Saturday?'

'Buy the ingredients and I'll make you a paëlla,' Angel said. 'It's my specialty.'

1962

Angel first learned to cook in the legionnaire's mess in Algeria. He passed the time experimenting with paëlla and other dishes, adding little touches he had seen his mother use. He also learned to smoke the short untipped cigarettes of dark tobacco he still prefers. The legionnaires waited. They played cards. The French Army was under attack from the French themselves. All that 'Week of the Barricades,' as it was later called, chaos reigned. There were rumors that some regiments of the French Army might refuse to budge if ordered onto the streets.

Sharing tagine from a large dish one night, Angel was reminded vividly of home, of his mother's kind eyes and his father's rough hands as they all dipped their bread in a dinner that was mostly sauce conjured with tasty care from few ingredients.

When the legionnaires had finished the *tajine* Angel went outdoors and sat on a hummock. He smoked, listened to a dog bark, and felt homesick.

Angel and his comrades trained, dozed, cooked, waited. This was not their war. What did Spaniards, East Europeans, and Germans care about firing on French people who sang the *Marseillaise* and shouted '*Vive l'Algérie Française*'? They told stories, about sixty-five legionnaires who resisted two thousand Mexicans in nineteenth-century Mexico and who, down to their last five survivors, had fixed bayonets and charged. Legionnaires were considered not men, but devils. They had captured Algeria for the French. When ordered, Angel and his comrades-in-arms would fire. They would serve France with honor. Most knew why they were in the Legion: passports, jobs, a better life. Some would make a career of it. Many were escaping their past. Most enjoyed the adventure. Only Angel had no ideas at all.

1980s

Angel abandoned his own garden to plant oleanders among the English couple's olive groves. An insect on the oleanders ate the beetles on the olive trees. He tidied terrace walls after rain and generally looked after things as best he could.

When old Boismal finally quit work because of his lungs, René Boismal Jr came to see Angel at rue Sans Nom.

'He's had it,' he said. 'You can hear him breathing in the next *Département.*'

They'd all heard about the effects of pesticides. One farmer wore an outfit like an astronaut when he went spraying.

'Papa never followed the rules,' René said. 'I learned my lesson the day I forgot my watch after spraying. Walked back down the line to get it and woke up flat on my back. Stuff knocked me out cold.'

'The watch still working?' Angel smirked.

René didn't laugh. 'I'm afraid the joke's over,' he said.

Angel had already guessed what was coming. 'I'm to be let go.'

'Look at it from my point of view,' said René. 'I can manage on my own with the machines now. And my son's coming up. Besides, the new vines I'm going to plant will take five years to come on.'

'You'll still have to prune 'em,' said Angel half-heartedly.

'I'd be glad to pay you by the hour occasionally. It's the social security no one can afford. I bought Maurin's next door, the whole lot is to be cleared.'

'No more slop,' said Angel with a curl of the lip.

René. nodded. 'I'll plant Chardonnay and Merlot and if they don't want to give them *Apellation Contrôlée* it'll be the best *Vin de Pays* in the world.'

'*Que conneria,*' said Angel.

They went to the café and drank a bottle of pastis between them. The next day Angel sent a sick note and stayed in bed for a week. He never worked for old Boismal again and the old man never left his house again, sitting alone coughing and wheezing noisily, watching the valley through a chink in the shutters.

51

1962-1965

Rodrigo wrote to Angel wherever he was stationed. He wrote of Gloria, now his wife, and of babies as they were born. The paper became less smudged, the writing firmer, more confident. 'I enclose photos,' Rodrigo wrote. The photos had different handwriting on the back with the children's names and three kisses, signed Gloria.

When Algeria finally got independence from France in 1962, Angel and his group went on to spend periods all over Africa and the French Midi: Djibouti, Madagascar and finally various barracks in Carcassonne, Castres, Castelnaudary.

On his walk away from the Legion, his new passport in his pocket, St Gervais du Bosc presented a physical barrier of some kind, stopped Angel on his inland walk, became his home away from home. If something was missing, Angel could not have defined it.

1985

Old Boismal's death marked other changes in St Gervais: Co-op wine slowly improved; more and more tourists came from the north, and some bought houses. Change didn't affect everyone: Simone continued to worry that late frost might ruin her peach harvest, handling the delicate fruit in her palm like a cloud. Old Marinette continued to tell of past floods and natural disasters. Many sold land to neighbors wanting to expand their vineyards. A gap began to show between the new farmers and the old. René Boismal Jr was one of many who lived in half-built new villas and worked their farms alone with machines and maybe an eldest son. 'Young people these days have no interest in farming,' he told Angel, 'they only want out—to bigger discos in Nimes or even Paris.' The hippies who had settled in the hills in the late '60s to make goats' cheese had finally gone back to the cities to earn money. A few ageing ones remained, drove big old cars or painted. 'They deal heroin,' René Boismal said.

No one wanted the old vines, especially those on difficult slopes that had to be harvested by hand. Angel's English friends were the only people still producing what Boismal called slop.

'Would you consider working for us full time?' they asked Angel, 'under the table, of course.'

Angel took from them less than it was worth, and drew unemployment benefit as well. He was able to send more money to Rodrigo. With the extra hours he got for helping Boismal Jr he bought two-tone jackets and peaked caps, which he sported in the evening at the restaurant or the café. 'The boys will continue their studies,' Rodrigo wrote. There were photos of a Spain Angel no longer recognized, with large white box-like structures sprawling along the coast and over the hills.

Angel shared any vegetables that still managed to grow in his own garden with the English couple, and stopped paying rent for the garden.

'They deserve it,' he said to the Englishwoman one evening as they sat together on the terrace. They'd being doing this for several evenings since her husband had left for England on business.

'Who?' she asked, turning the cool glass provocatively in her hands.

'The French,' he said.

She smiled.

'I wouldn't give you a centime for a Frenchman,' he said.

'Oh, come on,' she said.

'*Una mierda,*' said Angel. 'They think they're worth more than the rest of us. Do you want to become a billionaire?'

She waited.

'Buy a Frenchman for what he's worth and sell him for what he thinks he's worth.'

She read the Tarot cards for him, holding his hand in candlelight. There was a lot of talk about the Hanged Man. She pronounced his name Ann-hell, and giggled.

Never quite sure why the couple had been so friendly towards him, Angel was now very much at a loss to interpret this new attitude of hers. If anyone had asked, he'd have described himself as the man without a country from a street without a name.

After that he kept out of the Englishwoman's way until her husband returned, hiding on the terraces towards evening, watching tourists in shorts rush down the mountain, their legs torn from scorpion broom, their arms full of orchids and other rare plants that it was illegal to pull. He listened to the hammering at Boismal's house and the other new villas until it was time to go home.

1990

On his return, the Englishman announced that their son would not be back to continue work on the house. There had been some money disaster. The word equity was used a lot. Angel couldn't follow any of it although he gathered it was bad.

'We've decided to rent accommodation,' the Englishman said.

For a while Angel found himself assisting with interior arrangements, hanging curtains and carrying furniture. She was so preoccupied she did not confuse him with strange behavior and odd signals, and he liked her better that way.

Angel moved into the *mazet* at the foot of the vineyard nearest their house, and enjoyed living mostly outdoors again. He began to sport a full beard. The two-tone jackets became dirty and were abandoned. Summers were marked by listless people sitting around the pool, walking bareheaded in the afternoon, complaining about local habits and attitudes. 'Why don't the French...?' they would whine. Angel imitated them perfectly for René Boismal. 'Who burned Joan of Arc?' René replied. It wasn't a question.

'I'm going to stop taking grapes to the Co-op,' the Englishman announced one day. 'I want you to rehabilitate the old wine-press—a fine specimen and once the peak of village progress.'

Busloads of people came to taste and grimace. *Le Mas du Cirque* became synonymous with bad wine.

'Since when can the English make wine?' René Boismal asked, sitting on his tractor on the square, waiting for his lunch. 'When I hear talk of oak casks, I reach for my gun.'

'*Leche,*' Angel spat on the hot flagstones.

Changes came faster now. The Englishwoman took groups for painting holidays, and Sunday painters could be seen all over the village wearing shorts and drinking to excess in the evening. Many of them purchased small houses, drank the worst of the wine and generally boosted the local economy. Angel's fiftieth birthday was celebrated at the *Mas*, overlooking the finest view of the cirque and the valley, with a gigantic outdoors paëlla which he made himself, not talking much to anybody, just tending the giant dish on the fire. When people asked how he was, he replied *'Comme un vieux.'* Like an old man.

If anyone got into discussion with him after a few drinks, he said, 'If I'd done fifteen years in the Legion instead of five, I'd be retired now with a pension, anywhere I wanted.'

The Spanish families stopped coming to pick grapes. The largest local landowners brought in North Africans to live in the least attractive of the smaller houses and work in the fields, as people like Angel had once done.

In the autumn, carloads of students from the former East Bloc countries drove down for the grape-harvest. Angel and René Boismal watched beautiful, pale, blonde, creased young things pile out of cars on the village square. Angel wondered if farming in Valencia was under similar pressure. He imagined a world of displaced people—his schoolmaster once said there had been economic migrants even in Roman times.

'Economic migrants. Caught in other people's crossfire,' Angel muttered to René Boismal. René frowned and didn't reply.

1991

Prices rose, and the French dropped out of the holiday and house market, leaving foreigners the main source of income.

Then one day, a day like any other, the first Gulf War broke out and the world came to a standstill. Foreigners dried up. The international market crash followed. 'For Sale' signs went up everywhere. It was a while before the mood at *Le Mas du Cirque* was finally allowed to slip into despair. By then the English couple owed Angel four months' pay. He heard drunken quarrels in the night.

Angel wakes from a dream in which his mother is calling him to dinner across a surface of dark green water. He emerges from his *mazet* to find the two cars, the three dogs and their owners gone. The house is locked. A 'For Sale' sign hangs on the gate in three languages.

Angel knows his luck has run out.

For a long time no one will come to ask what he is doing there or if he has any right to draw water, grow vegetables, harvest olives. He will let the vines go wild. They'll be pulled up anyway, subsidized by government grants whenever a new owner is found. They will make roaring winter fires.

And some evenings, when he sits alone at the door of the little *mazet*, smoking and watching the sunset, he feels sorry for the vines: these gnarled, dry blackened things may be his only friends—unless you count the Arabs. Angel exchanges the odd word of Arabic with them. Dark, slight women with babies on their backs picnic among the vines, laughing, although they remain subdued in the village. Locals frown on noisy Arab children skipping in the shade of rue Sans Nom on summer afternoons. Angel pats the odd little head as he walks by. He doesn't joke about killing 'melons.' He doesn't go to the café or the restaurant. He no longer sends money to Rodrigo, who has probably made a tidy income from rentals on the coast. He knows Rodrigo and Gloria will not miss him, although it pleases him to think they may miss his money, now that business is bad in Spain too.

One of the Arab parents, Ahmed, has become a friend and visits regularly. He arrives now, carrying a packet of biscuits, puffed from the climb.

'*Qahwah*?' Ahmed nods and Angel goes about making coffee in the little *ibrik* his friend has given him. One of his few, treasured belongings, it doesn't require electricity.

Ahmed, passionate about words and their origins, draws from his jacket a notebook where he jots the links between Spanish and Arabic. He helps the local children with their lessons. He says the 'Bosc' in the village name is from Germanic and Latin roots and means 'wood.'

Ahmed and Angel study words together. Angel has learnt the Arabic origins of some everyday words, place names and institutions: he has learnt that Gibraltar comes from *Jbel Tarik*, the mountain of Tarik, the Berber who once invaded Spain, that Europe's oldest still- activemedical school in Montpellier, based its beginnings on writings of the Arab masters.

'But we have more than all that in common,' Ahmed says.

Angel slowly lifts his head from the coffee. 'We are the lowest forms of life in the village.'

Ahmed points upwards, one hand on his heart, 'And Allah watches out—'

'So that neither of us will resort to a big nail on a beam.'

Angel laughs.

They drink good, strong coffee.

Listening to Ahmed and looking out at the vineyards in the blinding sunlight, Angel doesn't marvel at the confusion and lack of purpose—other than eating and sleeping—of one small life. He repeats for his friend the proverb of the wise king, given him by his old schoolmaster as his only baggage before leaving home forever: *Old wood best to burn, old books to read, old wine to drink and old friends to trust.*

NIKODJE'S LAP OF HONOR

The psychologist Georg Groddeck once said that even breaking your leg was no accident. I'm going to tell you a story about my father, and you can decide for yourselves.

My father was utterly transformed, the day he brought home his Mercedes Benz. He always called it by its full name, even long before it ever seemed possible that he'd actually own one. It stood there that first day, dazzling on the cobblestones, in shocking contrast to the shaky masonry and loose drainpipes of the buildings surrounding our yard.

Up to then, I'd always seen him as an apologetic man, slightly bent over—he even appeared to have a slight hump, although there was no deformity of any kind—as if he was constantly expecting a blow from somewhere. He was the sort of man who went around objects and avoided confrontation. One of those very large objects was my mother. She ran the show.

My mother is the sort of woman who takes up a lot of space. I am an only boy, with no sisters to compare myself with but I sometimes imagine that I must resemble my father and that this displeases her. Yet my father and I always complied with her wishes, one of which was that I do my damnedest to try for a prestigious *Grand Ecole*. This looked extremely unlikely in those early days, given the quarter, the local schools teeming with immigrants like ourselves, the lack of French people and language. Yet it was an admirable goal too, and she followed, supervised and helped—in her supreme unknowingness—every step of the slog-hard way till I passed those very competitive entrance exams. I'm in. This autumn is my first year, and I'm enjoying it thoroughly, even if I miss my father. How he would have enjoyed all of it. He'd have been so proud of everything—from the kind of work we students do, to sailing weekends on the coast with friends. The fact that I was more or less off their hands, with a good grant as well, was one of the reasons he was able to afford the new car. I comfort myself by thinking that he went out in a blaze of glory.

My mother's apparent domination of him, and all those around her, is partly due to her job. It was she who found the job in France as *concierge* in the first place, probably she who pushed the plans forward and got them out of that infernal hole—'down home,' as they still call it. She put us on the map, you might say. She took over the job from a Portuguese couple who were heading home to realize their dream and live on a mountain up near Galicia, in a house they'd built themselves. Apart from my father's dream of one day owning a Mercedes, I don't know what other goals my parents had, back then.

It is unusual to have a Yugoslav guardian, most are Portuguese. Even though everyone now calls them *gardiennes*, the old enamel plaque on the wall, blue on white, still announces '*Concierge*' proudly, an echo of a past when this position was something to be proud of, before those old Parisian busybodies drove it into disrepute by snooping and spying on all and sundry. There is the occasional one like that left, but they get short shrift these days. They have to behave themselves or their Christmas box gets reduced—and it's not negligible, a tenth of a month's rent. Not that a name-change was necessary in our quarter of northeast Paris: there is little enough prejudice against us, the inhabitants are poorer than we are, and in any case my mother meets all derision head-on. I doubt there's anyone in the whole cube of buildings who would dare take her on.

Not that she didn't have plenty of natural curiosity. I often saw her peer around people into the apartment when she delivered the mail, and she had a way of asking the simplest of questions. One day I realized that all she really sought was someone to tell her story to. She wasn't sneaky either: she told people about all the apartments she and Father had bought and done up. The house in Brittany really impressed people, although you could see it was almost too much— farting higher than your arse, as the French say. Whenever someone called to our caretaker's lodge near the old carriage doors, I was reminded of the contrast between the smallness and darkness of this, their lifelong abode, and the various other ones they owned and rented.

Everyone was coming to France when my parents made their way here, back in the 1970s. France needed workers, Tito let them go. I must have been the product of those early years of euphoria, and they obviously weren't tempted twice. My mother ran the show, maintained a steady salary, delivered the mail to each door, kept residents in order and squalor to a minimum, cleaning stairs and sluicing out smelly communal toilets once a week, wheeling out heavy green bins at night. During all this, my father brought up the slack behind a sewing machine in whatever sweatshop had work going, sometimes all night if an order had to be produced quickly. He sewed sleeves for fancy suits for famous designer X, ribbons onto fur bobbles for famous designer Y, came home with his clothes covered in and coughing up the fluff of whatever fabric he'd been working on, kept a machine at home too, on which he did jobs for neighbors and friends and made scarves for children and zippered bags for sale in the markets from bags of offcuts.

The butt end of the rag trade has been changing recently. The ground floor workshops used to lie open onto the street, radio going full blast while foreign conversation, laughter and tears batted about. Nowadays machines hummed behind closed doors, and things are often run by the latest arrivals, the Chinese, whose workshops smell of rice and who never open doors, especially to anyone carrying a briefcase. Inscrutability and language incomprehension. At the post office, clerks spend half their time cashing refugee checks and helping the same people fill out postal orders for the folks back home. Just before the changeover to the Euro, the same post office was swamped by adolescents coming in relays to launder dirty money. There are rumors about the Triads, and trafficking in children. Who knows?

My mother at least learned to speak French, with an accent, while Father never took to either the people or the language, and hardly spoke a word of it at his death, twenty years later. His free time was spent in the Yugoslav cafes and restaurants round the quarter, places that stand out in their cleanliness and tidiness, and where the food and the television are focused on a greater Serbia, and where every shot of the wars in Bosnia and Kossovo was studiously followed, discussed, analyzed. It can't have been easy for him to hang around with other second-class citizens like himself, but then it can't have been easy for my mother either. She comes from proud peasant stock, people who always owned their own land and beasts, controlled their sources of income, people who kept themselves to themselves. My father was a townie. But whatever drew them together was stronger than what divided them, and they arrived in France together and never went back home once, in all the twenty years.

Until my father decided to drive his new Mercedes down there this summer.

It was early summer when he drove it into the yard. The sun glinted hotly off its dark sheen, and most of us circled it several times to get used to the feel of being near its greatness, before we examined the details or dreamed of sitting in it.

Father was in a frenzy of activity. He made his way time after time, over and back to the house for cushions, gewgaws to hang on the mirror, a bead thing for sitting on. Each time he made the journey he moved like a man in his own world, oblivious of us all, giving my mother a wide berth. She hung back, watching him with an amused smile on her face, pleased for him, but not really involved. In all the years they had bought, restored and rented apartments she had never seen him so satisfied. The real estate investments had been her pleasure. He'd gone along with it, humped bags of rubble up and down stairs, tiled and plastered and hammered in his spare time. They'd kept me away from all that, sure that I would never need to get my hands dirty. And throughout it all my father had talked and dreamed of one thing only: the day he would own a Mercedes Benz.

It smelt factory-new. Most of the hangers-on in the quarter had a sit in it before my mother and I were finally invited to hit the road for a jaunt. It struck me how youthful my mother looked when she was happy. She wears big skirts and has kept her hair long, and when the invitation finally came, I was surprised to notice her hesitantly finger her apron strings like a girl, unsure of herself. For the first time in my life I saw her confidence thrown, yet I think even this pleased her. I had the impression that my father got as much of a kick out of people's reactions to it as he would from actually driving the car, until I saw him behind the wheel.

Behind the wheel he began to unfold, like a morning flower. His shoulders straightened, he held his chin higher. The humpback disappeared. His hands on the controls were those of a confident multi-millionaire, someone who had this in his blood. From time to time he looked at us, smiling, as if to ask, 'What do you think?' or 'Not bad, eh?'

But he didn't utter a word. Words might have choked him. He slipped in and out of the traffic like a man who did it every day. Years of driving the old van around workshops and handyman stores helped, but nothing had prepared us for this style, this panache.

I had a new father, and Mother had a new man.

It wasn't long before he announced that he intended to drive down home, to their home place near the border with Kossovo. They had a month's holidays every summer, during which they usually faithfully headed off for Brittany, in imitation of the French. I could take or leave Brittany with its sunburnt tourists and its changeable weather, but I never dared complain given all they were doing everything for me. If I were to fail, I sometimes reminded myself, they would probably consider their lives to have been in vain.

It was then that I realized why they had never gone home, in all that time. Of course they were curious now to see how things really were, 'down home,' after all the bombing. There had been increasing talk of depleted uranium and how much of it had been spread about. But the real reason they had never ventured back, I realized now, was that they never felt themselves quite rich or presentable enough. By not getting involved with 'down home,' they had also avoided the cargo-ing back and forth of big plastic bags full of the produce needed down there or missed up here. They had escaped the shared concerns of sending money home, getting a lift home, finding a new and cheap way of phoning home (a phone booth on rue de Belleville functions without money, its location a precious well-known secret). Most of the immigrants, when the farm down home was completely equipped, went on to finance the restoration of the old house, then the new house. Since their own lives were sacrificed anyway, the emigrants were even beginning to finance a whole new generation coming along at home, in a variety of jobs from bakeries to more sweatshops.

My parents avoided all that, the endless yelling phone calls, the bitching, the whining, the discussions about how much it cost to repatriate the body. They never went home for holidays, never talked about home, and had gone for French nationality as soon as they were able. They seemed to take pleasure in the restoration work they did, and nothing pleased Mother more than showing people the work they had learned to do from scratch, pointing out details of tiling and wallpapering. You could see it wasn't everyone's taste, but it was neat and clean. They just grafted ahead with another apartment purchase, another renovation, all their money and energy tied up in that, and in me. When they started they couldn't stop, for they had never decided what the limits were to be.

The Mercedes, however, suddenly seemed to do the trick. I could see them becoming more and more enthusiastic about the idea of going home. They got out the maps and planned the journey and phoned people and arranged an itinerary. They would go via Austria and drop in on family there. Very soon the Mercedes was choc-a-block with stuff going to this one and that, including a dismantled sewing machine for a niece in Austria who was about to be set up on the path of the sewing life.

What had possibly set the Mercedes purchase in motion was a relatively harmless incident which had annoyed Father severely. One day he was sent across town to deliver a microscopic skirt to one of the big name designers. The van broke down, so he took the metro. Most people would have been glad of the excuse to take it easy for an hour or two. Not my father. He liked to work, at all times. One of his biggest criticisms of Albanians is that they just don't work: he called them *Sheptar*, a nasty down-home word for them that I knew he heard used often in the cafes roundabout. Mother disapproved of it, and every time he used it she would glance at me quickly and hiss 'Nikodje!' at him reprovingly, in a shocked voice.

What made the designer skirt episode worse was the insult

when he arrived at the designer's place on the other side—
the *rich* side—of town. His boss had forgotten to give him
the pattern that went with it. They were furious, probably
suspecting his workshop of making a hasty copy. And
maybe they had, although my father and mother severely
disapproved of anything dishonest. It probably goes on all
the time. Whatever the case, he then had to turn around and
come back across town again, pick up the minuscule pattern
and humbly make his way back with it. His boss refused to
pay for a taxi, and for some reason my father never dreamed
of rising up and paying for one with his own money. It was
a dull wet Parisian day. The metro was sluggish. He just
shunted over and back across town seething inwardly at the
way he'd been treated: the implication of dishonesty, the lack
of reliable transport, the role of go-between.

Or it could have been the incident with the Chinaman at
the dentist's, early that same morning. Mother had a tendency
to underline the nationality of the people she talked about.
Father simply grunted: *'Même pas français'* (They aren't even
French) was a frequent refrain of his. Sometimes it seemed
the only phrase in French that he knew.

Earlier that morning, a Chinese man—or a man Father
assumed to be Chinese and who could in fact have been
from anywhere between Mongolia and Japan and was most
likely Vietnamese—had closed the door in his face, the door
into the dentist's building. 'Can't let you in,' the man had said,
'ring the bell of the apartment you want.' Father had to ring
the bell again and wait till the dentist's secretary pressed the
button to release the catch. By that time Father was furious.
It wasn't so much the door, as the fact that it had been a

'foreigner' that had refused him entry. '*Même pas français*,' Father said dejectedly at dinner that evening. I didn't point out that many Vietnamese had probably been 'French' long before Father.

He must have ordered the new car straight away, because it arrived a month later. After the initial preparations and a couple of shorter jaunts, they were ready to try the *Périphérique*, the Paris ring-road, and head for home. My mother arranged for a neighboring *concierge* to take over her chores, and they dressed up and set off, complete with maps and picnic, abstemious to the last. They had refused extra passengers, so as not to make enemies.

It was a fine July morning. I didn't anticipate trouble. Rejoicing at having the place to myself for the first time ever and doing all the things normally forbidden, I was spreading myself around the kitchen. I hadn't washed the breakfast dishes. I was reading at table.

Suddenly the phone rang.

Mother sounded a bit shaky, but unhurt. She was calling from the main halls of a hospital.

Father had had a major coronary at the wheel, and had hit the side barrier going fairly fast.

Mother had been saved by airbags and comfort, but Father was gone. The car was a twisted write-off.

'Your father had his lap of honor, Christian,' she kept saying, 'Nikodje had his lap of honor. He died happy. We did a tour of the *Périphérique* before his heart exploded.'

Then she cried.

I told her to wait for me in the lobby of the hospital, and grabbed my coat.

MUSICAL INTERLUDE

It is eleven at night, a short walk from the centre of Paris. Suddenly, very loud rap music blasts from the open windows of the second floor of number 22, rue Saint Louis. Most people are already in bed; many of them get up and leave before dawn to head for sweatshops and building sites. Some heads appear in the few lighted windows, and wait.

After a while six young men appear on the street. They are known as Beurs, a name adopted for themselves by young people of North African families. Beur represents Arab, in *Verlan* or backwards slang. The young men whistle up at the noisy window, but of course they can't be heard over the music. As if by magic, a policeman appears in the doorway opposite. He watches and listens to the crackle of his walkie-talkie. It is only when the boys whistle and roar in concert that the head of another Beur like them finally emerges from the window with the noise. 'Are ye deaf or what?' the boys inquire. He looks down at them uncomprehendingly. They smile. 'Ye eejit,' says one of them, 'turn the goddamn music down!'

This is what the inhabitants hoped for: someone of the same generation to tell him. Better that than anyone from an older generation, someone he could, in his misery, accuse of being anti-Arab. For this is his reply to everything he sees, his sum and answer to the whole question of his daily interface with the world. 'You're afraid of Arabs,' he said one

70

day when eighty-seven-year-old Fernande negotiated around a parked car rather than step up on the high footpath beside him. 'I didn't even know you were Arab,' she had replied, astonished. It hadn't even occurred to her. For seconds, each had dragged the other back to the present: he had drawn her back into real life from a nightmare of aches and pains, dead friends, mourning her husband, administrative hassles. For an instant, Fernande had reminded him that not everyone thinks of things in terms of Arab and non-Arab, of 'them' and 'us.'

Still, it seems to him the pain of the others is somehow less than his own. His need to listen to Marseilles rap music at full volume may be explained by this and more: by his desire to hear and understand the words, those words of minority hurt. He wants to hear their pain and have his own pain explained to him. But what he hears is only the tip of the iceberg. And then the seldom time he turns up the music, he gets into trouble with half the neighborhood.

Now, while everyone watches and waits, the policeman finally lowers his walkie-talkie and says suddenly, 'Turn the volume down a bit.' The Beur at the window nods silently, and turns inside to lower the music. No one will ever know whether it is the presence of the policeman or the insistence of his own generation that carried the most weight, or how his pain may be appeased.

Even the policeman, it turns out, has other pain in hand: as the music incident is closed and people withdraw from windows to retire, they hear him say into his walkie-talkie, 'I'm at number seventeen, family row.' He pauses to listen for a crackling reply. 'Send me some help,' he says briskly but coolly. And the watchers realize that the rap music incident was a mere drop in the ocean of the night voyage through the streets of *Paris Est*.

A Parallel Life

Writing is a difficulty Zorica approaches tongue out, armed with the accoutrements she adores: paper clips, see-through file dividers, pens. The result is a single word, her surname. Although the letters look as if they are ready to be joined to others—as in infant school—they stand shakily alone. This is more or less how Zorica sees herself in the world of French bureaucracy.

French administration is a dragon to Zorica, its huge mouth occasionally and often inexplicably showering hot air and flames in the shape of Orders to Pay and bailiff's letters. Even a French electricity bill comes with the proviso that if it isn't paid within a fortnight, it will be increased by ten percent. Zorica keeps careful and fearful watch for the dragon, signing her surname painstakingly on checks that others have written for her. In my absence the lady who works in the post office accepts two Euros for this job, for Zorica prefers her financial affairs to remain secret from our other neighbors. When I write a check for her, we sometimes have to scrap the whole operation while Zorica starts her signature again, tut-tutting loudly.

When you can only write one word, you want it to be perfect.

She is illiterate, she says, because of the war. World War II covered her school-going years, when Zorica's reading and writing abilities must have seemed a minor priority in a devastated Mitteleuropa. Her neighbor and fellow countryman, Srboljub, on the other hand, cannot write, Zorica says, 'because of his head.' A brutish giant of little sensibility, he exercises his cunning on the French to great advantage, claiming unemployment benefit and rent allowance while working on the black, and thousands of francs from the insurance for regular leaks on his fly-specked ceiling. If an inspector turns up to check, he shrugs ignorance of any known language. Zorica says he murdered his father. 'The tractor turning over wasn't an accident,' she said. 'He wanted to get married again.' Then she smiles: 'If he'd been a Kossovar, he could've had as many wives as he wanted!' Another version of the story is that the father died of shame at his son's reproaches: it just wasn't fair, Srboljub said, buying a new tractor for his sister, while he wore his butt out in Paris.

From a faded photograph, Zorica's own father smiles down at us from underneath a huge white moustache, the sort of man easily imagined goading a mule from the bench seat of a cart sporting car tires, on a dusty road in flat country, somewhere east of Austria.

Zorica lives in a world parallel to the one the rest of us inhabit, where everyone is a potential enemy intent on some devilry. She is convinced that the husband of another neighbor was killed by the doctor because he was from Serbia. The hospital asked first, she swears. 'Are you a Serb or a Croat?' they asked. 'I'm a Yugoslav,' replied the husband, who was close to being discharged. But they knew. He was taken away and given an injection. Next day he was dead, says Zorica.

Zorica maintains that a Croat doctor refused to treat her during the bombing of Yugoslavia, because she was from Serbia. The doctor had herself replaced. I said this was impossible, in France, and should be reported. 'Non,' Zorica said firmly, 'I want no trouble about it.'

The world around Zorica is so nasty in intention that she sometimes resorts to visiting a lawyer who, like her doctor, is from the same region as herself and clearly takes advantage of the situation to pour oil on troubled waters for a minuscule fee, making her angrier than warranted by whatever administrative process is in hand.

When something does go wrong that must be righted, Zorica's frustration is palpable, her angers volcanic, her voice raised to maximum, her precious little French deserting her. She shouts and shouts 'Non, Non, Non!' louder and louder against all arguments, until finally her interlocutor gives up in despair. In the administrative offices of the quarter you only have to pronounce her name and they sigh.

Even a map makes little sense to Zorica. As she peers over my arm, I suddenly see her as an ancient Greek, gazing at the map of a Pytheas or a Ptolemy, wondering at this thing that they call the 'known world.' Such maps bear no relation to Zorica's Europe, furnished with the routes and contacts that she has memorized in order to get around. I am sure she could find her way home on foot, if she had to, across four countries. Paris is measured by her own gauge of offices, shops and people she knows or needs to know, travelling on the bus—for in the metro one travels not only underground but notionally, towards destinations that are mere words. Above ground, Zorica needs no such esoteric skills, and can even persuade bus drivers to let her out where she wants and not where they should stop. All of her sorties are connected with some mission or other, and she only notices Paris amusing itself when she accidentally comes upon it. One summer evening we stumble on an open-air concert in Parc de la Villette. The spectators loll on the grass, 'Like seals on a beach in the Galapagos,' says Zorica, who studies wildlife on afternoon TV.

She lives in a tiny room, with the use of a communal toilet on the stairs. When in a foul mood, she says, 'I live like a tramp.' Her TV is perched high up near the ceiling, on a shelf disguised with a lace veil that cunningly conceals the video beneath. Anything that can be interpreted as a shelf has a handmade lace curtain hanging from it. Shelves develop from shelves and cascade down the walls to just above the level of two industrial sewing machines that squat along one wall, their enormous cotton spools still in place, appropriately enough in red, white and blue: imperialist, French colors. Any empty areas are filled with plants that crawl up the walls, across the ceiling and out the window, where they run to meet lively geraniums in giant pots on the ledge below, contributing to the leaks and damp that plague the building. Beyond the flowers she has arranged a shaky set-up for drying clothes that often finish up on the street below. The unemployed young men hanging around the street bring them up and knock on the door. 'They're nice,' she says, which is not what she said when some of them shouted 'Yugoslav in a wig' when NATO bombing of Yugoslavia was in full swing.

When she smiles, she looks younger, especially when

the wig has been combed and put on properly, and not lopsidedly applied in response to a knock on the door. It has saved her a fortune in hairdressers' fees after chemotherapy made her own hair fall out. On bad days the TV helps her pass the time. When she has a headache, she soaks a white turnip in home-made rakia, then applies a facecloth soaked in the solution to her forehead. '*Doktures*,' she says, 'what do *doktures* know?' She makes liters and liters of lemon juice mixed with water and kilos of sugar, saying, 'It's good for what's wrong with me.'

When alone, she lies on the bed watching *Sunset Beach* and *Arabesque*. Good-looking men are excusable for their sins: 'Ah, Mikaël!' she laughs indulgently about one of the doctors in *Melrose Place*. Her solitary existence is peopled with characters from American soaps and, if given any encouragement, she can recount episodes from years back, like ancient epics.

But people are a welcome distraction, and the high point of a good day is when she has someone in for iced tea and it's time for the soaps as well. As she shows visitors out, reluctantly, after tea and homemade cakes, she apologizes, as if they were leaving because her room is too small: '*Excusez-moi, mon appartement est trop petit.*'

The single bed just shows under a rail of clothes that Zorica made herself. You can tell by the professional once-over she gives yours that she knows the qualities of good fabric, of work acceptable to top couturiers. After she got to know me well, she described being asked to take innocent photos at big fashion events, which turned out to be for immediate copying in illicit sweatshops. When she dresses up to go out, it is clear that her clothes are professionally made.

In a hat and sunglasses she looks a million dollars, suddenly out of step with her small room. She spends any spare coins on cheap luxuries like ice-cream pots in plastic, each with its own matching spoon in imitation biscuit and lurid pink, or candle-holders from Turkey in which tiny boats rise and fall on a vivid green sea trapped forever between plastic walls. There are multi-colored balls that act as ice-cubes for the iced tea she keeps ready in a bottle with painted flowers. When in form, she trawls the shops for such treasures for herself, or friends at home who've seen and coveted them, sometimes regretting that a gewgaw spotted and ordered by a neighbor or friend can't be repeated. Her bedside table, hand-made lace to the ground, is a cascade of informers' scraps bearing scribbled names of shops where such objects may be found. She can remember exactly what each corresponds to, getting literate visitors to confirm. Administrative pieces of paper, however, behave like white mice, and in spite of her stationery fetish and careful stapling, clipping and filing, they very often finish up attached to other entirely irrelevant documents, upside-down or back to back, mislaid forever.

When Tito set her free, she came to Paris with her remaining small son, whom she describes as a 'penalty goal in the final minute of play,' born after her husband died. In her heyday she worked lengthy days, falling exhausted under the machine for the night, as many still do in the sweatshops roundabout. The rag trade is like that, she says, when an order has to be produced quickly you just stay at it till it's done. Later the company gave her a room above the workshop, and the little boy played at her feet before finally going to a local school.

Since her arrival, Zorica has lived in a quarter where Serbs, Poles, Arabs and Jews work and drink together, hurling colorful insults at each other from the cafe on the corner. Pedestrians and cars stop and chat to sweatshop workers inside the bars of ground-floor windows. Only the Chinese seem to stick to themselves, getting drunk in their own bars, and working in their own sweatshops, which always smell of the rice-cooker in the corner.

Now that Zorica can no longer work, she can't sell her machines for what she paid for them, and would like to take them to Yugoslavia, now that things are very expensive down there. She never initiates conversation about the Yugoslav war, but in reply to enquiries about the family, says, 'They're not as badly off as some, they've got the farm, they won't go hungry.' There is some talk of 'dust' after the 'bombs' which is making people sick and has done strange things to the fruit. Yet one evening when a TV program about depleted uranium is broadcasted, she watches a romantic comedy on another channel. She is in two minds whether it is wise to go home, now the country's in such a state. Her basic French pension is some four hundred Euros, which the dragon might allow her to receive in Yugoslavia. The problem would be medical costs and care.

Once grownup, her literate and multi-lingual son went home to marry and run the farm. Now he has children too. His daughter recently married, and Zorica always shows new visitors the wedding videos, hours and hours of very serious-looking people, lean and handsome older men in hats, dancing hand in hand round a farmyard to the sound of great music—and Zorica likes it at maximum volume, bursting through the room and out the flower-drenched window. All the grandchildren are dark and good looking, one boy had just completed military service when war broke out. There is a suggestion that his military service was a nightmare of sleeping out in the damp and cold for weeks on end, but the family also paid 3,000 Euros to a colonel to keep him out of the war. They visited the colonel's house some twenty-eight times, bearing money and requests: 'It is a lot of money, but Antonije's life is more important,' she says.

In the video background lies the family house, with garlanded gates and a man-made pond that Zorica calls the *piscine*. Old cartwheels and planks have been used to make a garden seat painted red and white. 'Before, we had only horses and carts,' Zorica begins, then her eyes glaze over as she talks of her mother smoking hams and putting walnut leaves among the laundry, in beds and under carpets, against insects. 'Once,' she says, 'the Seine between Yugoslavia and Romania froze over—kilometers wide—and my grandparents went to Romania by sleigh.' All big rivers are the Seine to Zorica. I decide she is talking about the Danube. 'When it's cold like that, no one gets sick,' her grandfather told her.

Sometimes she improvises strange tales that reveal a primitive instinct sufficient to make the hairs stand on the back of my neck— 'Sasha was walking down the road one day when he met a strange woman with a horse's head...' she goes, or: 'Natasha looked into the cave. There was a bad, animal smell....' She watches me carefully for reactions. On the street, everyone is good for an invented story. She indicates a middle-aged man hovering, and says, 'Poor thing, she's stood him up.'

Sometimes if I use a farming metaphor or turn of phrase from my own past, I can pass completely through the barrier of language and find myself on the same side as a giggling Zorica who repeats her own word for winkers or spancels, amazed that such communication is possible at all, and vaguely embarrassed to find that it is, in the heart of Paris.

'Big wedding,' I nod toward the noisy video. 'Four hundred,' Zorica shouts above the music. Different outfits had to be made and worn for each day, she says proudly, enumerating just how many lambs and calves and chickens and geese had to be slaughtered to feed the crowds. 'Lot of money,' I say, rubbing thumb and forefinger together in the meaningful continental way, thinking of the expense of a wedding these days. 'No,' Zorica says firmly, 'the wedding meal is held at home, and since all the food is home-produced—you only have to buy Orangina.' Many of the band are family members, playing a mixture of Serbian, Gypsy and Romanian melodies.

Some people, of course, might just sit whining because they didn't have the money for a big wedding. That, Zorica seems to say, is one of the differences between Serbs and Albanians. But the biggest difference is that Albanian women don't work. 'Serb women *work.'* In fact, she says, 'Serbs in general *work all the time.* They come home from the day job and then they drive the tractor and feed the pigs: men, women, children.' The farm is—as farms once were in France— mixed, with all kinds of livestock and cereals, and require all hands to keep it going. Antonije called her only yesterday evening and said, 'I'm off out to do a bit of ploughing now, Grandma.' That's why Serbs are able to live on little, she says, because they work hard, and grow everything they eat.

'There's land in Albania,' says Zorica firmly, 'but they do nothing with it.'

They're not the only ones, she adds: Croatian women don't work either, they just wear a lot of make-up and spend their husband's money shopping, when they're not having babies.

Eventually, in the early 1980s, the firm that provided Zorica's job and lodgings closed down. By then she'd saved up enough to purchase her small room with its tiny kitchen alcove. She did most of the restoration work herself, showing no fear of plumbing or plastering. The little kitchen window, whose rotten frame prevents its shutting properly, overlooks a nineteenth-century yard in black and white and grey, straight out of Zola.

After years of contributing to the economy—even if it was only adding the label 'Made in France' so that a garment could be described as such and re-exported—Zorica fell far short of some French standard of perfection, hobbling through the last few years of illness on the newly-invented 'minimum wage' which, as she says, 'Wouldn't keep a healthy appetite in spaghetti.' This was backed up by the Town Hall for bills and other occasionals. They explained that if necessary they could give her extra money on the basis that when she died, her room would go to the Town Hall. She noted the name of her Town Hall interlocutor: Souad. 'No Muesli Man will tell me what to do,' Zorica replied. And with a keen sense of value, and property ('five thousand Euros to repatriate the body,' she once informed me) Zorica told the Town Hall she would prefer her family to inherit her room. So she shops carefully, and often eats spaghetti.

Over the years she became friendly with her social worker—for the French system requires that someone in Zorica's position throw herself on its mercy. The social worker was black, married to a white man, their children a pale chocolate color. 'She showed me photos,' Zorica laughs, 'I said, "What are you showing me these for? They can't be yours!"'

The day she reached retirement age, we celebrated with iced tea and bad wine. At last, she has a tiny pension. The social worker came, took a shot of wine, winced and explained that her role was finished. From here on, Zorica was on her own.

When NATO finally decided to bomb the Serbs, Zorica prefaced comments with a placatory, 'I know I live in France,' then continued, 'but they didn't have to bomb the place to bits.' She became very annoyed when a Romanian friend said, 'Kossovo's early gone. Next thing we'll take your region back too.' Zorica put her out, and hasn't spoken to her since. She becomes more impatient with all and sundry. When she is disturbed late one night by young people looking for her neighbor— 'Fabien won't answer the doorbell,' they tell her, 'he must be asleep.' She gives them a long, vicious look: 'And I don't sleep at all, I suppose?'

She is a great-grandmother now—photos of the recently-arrived and dark-eyed twins Nikodje and Tatiana are produced and pored over. She stays on in the little room watching soaps and waiting for phone calls, dozing more often.

When the war was all over, she wondered why the opposition didn't immediately make moves to replace

Milosevic, although she reckoned some of them weren't much better, since they were responsible for the loss of Bosnia. All she could do was watch and wait. When Clinton came up with the idea of putting a price on the head of Milosevic, she threw up her hands in despair: 'They'd all be surprised if someone put a price on Clinton. Yet he behaves like an ayatollah and nobody says a word....'

There is a census down home. Family members have to say whether they are Serb, Croat, Albanian or Romanian.

'So what did they put?' I ask.

'Serb, of course,' she replies with a little smirk that I do not understand.

When at last Milosevic is ousted, something changes in Zorica. She opens up and tells jokes about him that were current during the war and the elections, but which she never told before, in which Milosevic is a farmer who gets his pigs out to vote for him at election time.

She is going great guns until the dragon comes to life again: a minor administrative incident gets blown out of all proportions and she gets so worried that she cannot sleep. Her blood pressure soars. In the quarter, she has seen too many people shunted out of their modest rooms by unscrupulous building managers, for the minuscule sum of their overdue monthly charges. She recounts that one room was purchased for the equivalent of one thousand Euros, then sold on to a speculator. She refuses to believe that things have changed much, and she may not necessarily be wrong. She and many of her fellow countrymen confuse the ill-pronounced French name for building manager (*Syndic*) with the word for the organism that pays the dole (*Assedic*), lumping public and private French administration into one giant monster.

Whatever the case, change is in the air. More and more property changes hands in the quarter. Drilling and hammering are frequently heard. French bobo-lilies (young bohemian liberals) are moving in. The building manager has produced improvement estimates for a fortune, and if the other owners agree, Zorica would be obliged to cough up too. Public money may be available, but it's all too vague just yet. The situation escapes her. She can't keep up with the bills, and builds herself into a frenzy of worry.

After days of storming at the dragon, roaring at people in offices all over the quarter and even visiting her lawyer, it emerges that she had misunderstood a letter received during my absence. In her world, honest people are bigger to begin with, and when they fall, they fall hard and forever. Dishonest people are huge evil beings, dragons before which poor small people like her can only huff and puff and threaten with heroic language, or a magic sword.

Non et non et non. Je dis NON.

She doesn't lose the fight, but she doesn't win it either. Something is broken in her, and she decides she must go home. It is not said that this will be final, but it is unlikely that she will ever return.

The night before she leaves there is a film on television, set among east European gypsies. I phone her to switch over to it. She says 'Come on over and we'll watch it together.'

It is here, among heavily-laden luggage which she has been packing for days, that I make a final step towards the real Zorica. She understands some of the language in the film. I have missed the start, and ask her where it is set.

'Moldova,' she says firmly, 'where all the gypsies come from.'

There are several gypsy languages in Yugoslavia, she says. Her grandchildren can speak them, from playing music all over the country.

Then she looks at me as if she has made a decision.

'My people speak Vlah,' she says. 'We are Vlah.'

'So what language is taught at school?'

'The children are all taught Serb at school.' *Srb*. She pronounces it with a rolling 'r' and no vowel. It seems to me she says it with something of contempt. *Srb*. No one in her family can write Vlah, but she is the only one who cannot read and write Serb. Her son's generation was forbidden to speak Vlah at school. The Vlah minority in another region, Voivodine, got some minimal rights, but her own region is smaller, its minority dangerous because next door to both Bulgaria and Romania. 'They're afraid the neighbors might want it back!' she laughs.

I see in a new light her defense of the Serbs during the war, and her comments on Croats and Albanians.

'Bed-time,' she announces. 'We'll be loaded up like *bourricots* in the morning.' She giggles.

We await her bus on the broad boulevard, surrounded by bags overflowing with disposable nappies, sunflower oil, fine white flour and sugar. Her son has paid for the ticket at the other end—half a month's pension for her—and tipped the bus driver to look after her. Occasionally Zorica fiddles with the contents of several open shopping bags, fretting over them, transferring contents between them, occupying herself until the bus arrives. Cakes that Proust would have known as *madeleines* jostle with bottles of water, and a long naked doll in plastic molding peeks from under a towel. The trip home means she will see the new great-grandtwins.

It is bright and early July, the start of paid holidays for the great majority, a day when those whose holidays are over will head north from the beaches of the Mediterranean and most of the others who can afford to will leave Paris to take their places. French TV has warned everyone who can to stay off the roads. Here, for the moment, all is quiet save for small knots of preoccupied-looking people—mostly elderly and middle-aged—surrounded by gigantic suitcases and reinforced plastic bags. A few locked buses stand by, some with trailers. There is little traffic. Paris is still asleep.

Zorica pushes her way into most of the groups, asking questions, before electing to settle with one, which includes several middle-aged women of enormous size. It is a question of the name of the company as well as the destination of the bus, she explains. All the buses will head east out of France before crossing Bavaria, Austria, Hungary and branching off to their various destinations in the former Yugoslavia. The journey will take two days and a night. The group she eventually chooses is from the same region as hers, across the mountains and looking east into Romania and the sweep of the Carpathian plain, its back turned to Yugoslavia proper.

'You see,' her gesture envelopes the others, 'we're all Vlah, we don't even speak Serb.' Then she adds loudly, in case I haven't got it, 'Not Serbs.'

The others smile broadly.

She begins to fret again, nervous about the quality of the bus. She complains of someone who'd come the day before looking for stomach tablets for the journey, the same ones she gave them last year.

'Nothing would do them only eat at the first restaurant when we crossed the border,' she explained, 'so they were all sick and I had to give them tablets. Restaurants. Pah!'They should eat what they brought with them, like everyone else. 'Tablets, indeed. You don't waste precious tablets on idiocies like that.'

The crowds begin to gather now; vans, taxis and even minibuses have been hired to bring the passengers and their gigantic cargoes to the impromptu bus terminus. Drivers double-park at random then head off to smoke and chat with friends and acquaintances. Cries of 'Ho!' ring out. Shoulders are thumped and jokes abound, mostly among the men. The women just watch. By now my Vlah are lost among the Serb-speakers. People address me in languages I do not recognize, and I remember how lost I was when travelling in countries like theirs, where I could make a shot at none of the languages or dialects, where I was as lost linguistically as Zorica is alphabetically in France.

The sun grows warmer. Swarthy men with long hair and vivid red string vests jump out of a Renault and unload fat women and very pretty children. A young man with a clipboard comes by, but knows less than Zorica about when their particular bus will arrive, or where. More and more people wander from group to group in search of their bus. The few young people around openly show their dislike of the whole mess. One young man mutters that it is a circus.

By eight a.m. the drivers have congregated in a circle, smoking cigarettes, comparing notes and laughing. Many of them carry cartons of Gauloises cigarettes. Most of them are Yugoslav, but are speaking excellent French with a short Moroccan driver who regales them with stories of his last trip through. The Austrians were the worst. He mimics himself walking from one uniformed man to another: 'I go another few yards and it's *"Pass bitte!"* again.'

'Just how many times do you want to see it?' he says, in patient imitation of Austrian precision. He seems rather proud of just being able to cross all those borders with impunity, odd man out and brown to boot.

More people with clipboards appear. Traffic builds up as the newest arrivals triple park. Fresh buses wait for the drop-off vehicles to leave—or even for their drivers to re-appear—so they can park. French drivers on their way to work become impatient and irate, but nothing can kill the good humor of these people on their way home. Three policemen, obviously pressed into service for the occasion, take one look at the chaos and walk quickly by.

By the time the buses are due to leave, the drivers have unlocked the baggage compartments and the men with the clipboards begin to call the names of villages and passengers. Baggage is loaded in some kind of geographical order. Zorica's bus turns out to be an aged red and black affair with matching faded window curtains.

Her baggage carefully stowed, she embraces me and goes on board. A man in a flashy blazer with brass buttons, watching the chaos benevolently, breaks into chat with me.

Speaking good French, he is obviously an intermediary, the man who oils real and figurative wheels at borders. The buses don't travel together, he says, but they try to meet up regularly. In spite of having several drivers per bus, frequent stopping is obligatory, something he seems to regret. The Austrians are sticklers for paperwork, he confirms, but the Hungarians are worse—they just say, 'Why should we put up with you lot going through here?' and demand cigarettes and *baksheesh* at every turn. You got used to it. Sometimes three Euros was enough. Then it would be into Yugoslavia and home.

'First thing they all want to do is stop and have a meal, so we usually stop at a big service station just across the border.'

'What are the roads like?' I ask politely, noting that Zorica has already changed seats three times.

'They've rebuilt the bridge just over the border,' he says. He seems sure I must know the bridge in question, the one on stilts. 'Completely rebuilt with a new monument to those dead in the war.' All the bridges are rebuilt, he said. They started building them the day after the bombing stopped. 'They thought they could bomb us out of existence—it took them two months—oh sure, they killed people, they damaged buildings and tactical places, but they didn't put us out of action.'

I reflect on the audacity of it, and recall Milosevic announcing they would rebuild the country on their own, without any western aid, thank you very much. The man in the blazer shifts his shoulders and moves from one foot to the other.

'I wasn't for Milosevic,' he said. 'Before the war started,

I only kept half an eye on what was going on down there. But now, I realize what he did for the country. No outsider should come into a fight between neighbors. They're all afraid of civil war now. Before, the government supplied diesel for our tractors, but now there's either none at all or it's the same price as in France—in a country where salaries are six times lower!'

He became quiet again.

'It's okay now, but it's not okay, know what I mean? I have a neighbor whose twin sons, soldiers, were killed in Kossovo: one in the morning, one in the afternoon. When the Americans and English were supposed to be "negotiating" in Rambouillet, they already knew they were going to start bombing a few days later. It was decided already.' He suddenly became animated. 'And why do you think the Americans moved in? Because they wanted the ports, for the day they turn against Russia again. Now they're in, but Russia is penniless, for the moment. And Russia never liked Yugoslavia too much anyway. But just wait till they have some money!'

'What a waste of time and energy,' he says finally, 'and what a fool that Slobo is—he could have retired years ago and be fishing now.'

He calms down again and smiles indulgently at the efforts of helpers to pack in the gigantic bags. 'We ask them to say how many bags they'll have,' he says, 'and they do. But nobody ever mentions the size.' You could get everything in Yugoslavia, he adds, but they liked to bring stuff home anyway. A new passenger arrives with a barrel of cooking oil. 'There is a shortage of sunflower oil,' he admits.

Finally Zorica settles for a seat beside a lady of her own age, and I see that she is already gone from us, wrapped into another world.

The Moroccan gets into the driver's seat of the red and black bus. At last bus engines fire to life. The watching crowd reels backwards from the smoke that belches from the rear, laughing. The Moroccan tries valiantly to put it into reverse, without success. After some trilingual discussions, the man in the blazer sends for a driver from another bus. A thin elderly grey-haired man in an old-fashioned suit appears. Looking more like a bank manager or Samuel Beckett than a bus-driver, he is obviously the expert on either this bus or reverse gear, or both. He slips the gears into reverse without too much trouble. The Moroccan takes his place again, puts it into forward gear, moves out a bit, has several tries at reverse again without success.

It is hot work, before a crowd of onlookers, and there is no power steering. The grey-haired man takes over and demonstrates again, his face a mask of concentration. He explains the problem to the Moroccan, in French. This goes on for some time.

Finally the Moroccan jumps out of the bus and makes a long gesticulatory speech that there is no way he is going to drive this red and black heap all the way to Yugoslavia. A conference of drivers is held, and the grey-haired Beckett is commandeered. He noses the bus out. Then the Moroccan takes the wheel again. Now that traffic is moving again, the three policemen reappear and begin to direct it. Zorica blows kisses and mouths '*Au revoir*' through the window. Her new bus friend smiles and waves too. With great difficulty the bus

92

finally moves out into the holiday traffic around ten a.m.

I wonder what will become of the two sewing machines she left behind, and guess that a relative will come, dismantle and transport them home, coping somehow with the difficulties presented by the various customs dragons.

For the moment, Zorica has broken with one dragon, the French one. She leaves for home riding on another. I watch the red and black monster, with its forward and reverse drivers, limp off eastwards with its wake of black smoke.

As she said, its passengers are neither Serbs nor Romanians, they are Vlah, but above all emigrants and, like all emigrants, they are a generation sacrificed, returning home to what some like to call Greater Serbia.

After walking about for a while I have lunch and wander back to the quarter. It is late afternoon. Fitful showers hiss in the evening heat, mixed with a whiff of blocked drains. Some Polish builders have finished up a job and are piling their gear into the back of a van before heading for the *Périphérique* and home to Poland, enough money in their pockets to finance six months' living, or the purchase of a new truck. People who can't afford holidays sit watching the trendy young on the cafe terraces. A bicycle hangs neatly from a fourth floor window, out of thieves' range. The Asiatic evangelical meetinghouse on the corner disgorges the post-homily and post-prandial homeless. A few tramps congregate on a bench around a cheap bottle from the supermarket. *Concierges* wheel out overfilled green bins that are quickly and surreptitiously joined by piles of building rubble and sacks of offcuts from the sweatshops.

As I arrive at our building I find our *concierge*'s husband, Mr Dafonseca, sweeping the yard cobbles listlessly with a broom. He nods to me and indicates the mountains of rubbish. 'Now *there's* a nice neighborhood for you,' he says, with all the irony his pencil moustache can muster. His son's wife, an illegally-resident Algerian, wheels their new baby Augusto out for a ride in his buggy. The unemployed young men, including Dafonseca *fils*, play around with Mr Dafonseca's Rottweiler and prepare to sell hashish for the evening. They upbraid the younger kids for letting off firecrackers at their feet: *'Nique ta mère!' 'Dégage!' 'Connard!'* The kids are delighted.

The firecrackers mean it will soon be July 14, when the quarter comes alive in an uncharacteristic celebration of French feeling. Mr Dafonseca's daughter-in-law will salsa up the street in a red djellabah like the Pied Piper, ahead of a Batuk band and a dancing crowd of all ages. People will throw confetti from upstairs windows. Cameras will flash. Mr Dafonseca and his wife will lie in bed listening to the band, one ear out in case the young Augusto is disturbed by the noise of the throng. Upstairs, the Tunisians will rattle their backgammon board, smoke and chat. An elderly *pied-noir* Frenchman will belly-dance on a street enveloped in the whirling smoke of barbecuing *merguez*. A Serb will pass around a bottle of home-made *rakia*. Young North Africans will sell cheap cans of beer from buckets of iced water. Black tots in ribboned plaits will shake to the rhythms of an Italian band. The band will finish up an electric selection of folk tunes with an Italian anti-fascist song that goes, 'We're drunk, but we're coping!'

Zorica will no longer smile down on it all from her window,

across the flowers. She has seen her last fourteenth of July in this quarter that is a microcosm of the New Europe, and even a brave new world.

Down home, her great grand-twins, caught between two worlds, will play at blowing out the electric table lamp, giggling.

The older boy will sit at a computer, preparing an essay for school.

'Serbia is at the gates of Europe,' he will read from the Internet. 'If they catch Mladic, we'll get into Europe!'

'We've been in Europe all along,' Zorica will sigh, eyeing the giggling girls. She will stop sewing and switch off the table lamp.

'There you are girls,' she will say, 'you've blown it out now.'

Between Men

'Clouds sitting on my nose,' the estate agent told a Paris colleague on the phone. In Paris, they always thought people in the south should be out sunning themselves. Whenever northerners said, '"I hear the sun in your accent,' he almost threw up.

The village, indeed the whole region, was quiet, the affairs of summer packed away for another year. Vines had been pre-pruned and pruned once, some twice, ploughed and treated with some lethal yellow muck.

The phone rang. It was a client called Loison. 'I've a house to sell, up in Ste Eulalie,' Loison said.

The estate agent took the details, tidied his desk and left the office. He bumped into his secretary who was returning from lunch.

'You can close up if I'm not back,' he said.

On a day like this nobody would leave home unless he had to. The sun might reappear at intervals to warm the yellow and black stone villages, but this was the depth of winter darkness. He knew someone who, on days like these, went to bed and stayed there until spring beckoned again. The estate agent reckoned his own stiffness was a slight bout of rheumatism brought on by the damp. Either that or the force of gravity was beginning to pull harder. Keep it upbeat, he told himself: a damp day was ideal for showing up all the disadvantages of an old house.

He got his car from the large underground car park underneath his office, which was on the main shopping street, to attract stragglers, and drove off into the country. He decided not to turn on the radio, but instead marveled at what green remained, and would remain all winter: umbrella pines, dwarf oaks. Some old walls still displayed late oleander and bougainvillea. As he approached the little village—once and still more or less fortified—he appreciated yet again its lines and its age, although he knew he couldn't live there.

The streets were so narrow the only parking was on the village square, where two men on a mechanical hoist were tinkering with Christmas lights on a huge tree.

As he made his way on foot he realized that most people were by now dozing by the fire after lunch. The acrid smell of wood smoke hung in the air.

He followed Loison's instructions carefully, since none of the street names were marked. Sometimes people didn't know their new street name anyway, referring rather to someone who had once lived there, usually by a nickname: Marmite's house, Mosquito's lane, Pepe's alley. The names lived on after the death of their owners. The estate agent thought this might be a bit odd. A guest Buddhist, on a half-heard radio show in the car the evening before, had casually mentioned that the ego didn't exist. He himself had often noticed the meaningless air of a house whose owner had died or departed. And now they were saying the ego mightn't exist either. Were the locals desperately fighting the loss of Marmite and Mosquito's ego?

Concentrate, he thought. Business. Houses.

Dark damp stains shadowed the ground floor level of

most of the buildings, and would likely stay there until the sun warmed things up again.

He was beginning to think he'd gone wrong when he came on it: a dead-end street about a meter wide, a few stone houses on either side, each slightly different from its neighbor. The Loisons' house was taller and skinnier than the others, all dark because most of the stone was local basalt. Blue workmen's trousers and jackets hung from the balcony next door. Opposite, by way of reply, one huge pair of greying underpants hung from a makeshift wire under a window.

The estate agent knocked on the Loisons' door.

He had disturbed a late lunch which the Loisons were eating in a triangular room whose two street windows provided the only natural light.

Mme Loison was feeding potato croquettes to a bald parrot in a cage on the table. The cage door was open but the grey-fleshed parrot was so busy inside that the estate agent thought at first it must be engaged in some kind of acrobatics. The parrot held onto its perch with one claw and reached the croquette up to its beak with the other, its grey baldness exaggerating what was already comical enough. The estate agent had a dreadful urge to laugh, which he drowned with difficulty.

The Loisons offered him food, coffee, anything he wanted. 'I had a sandwich early on,' he said.

He could see the performance going on all afternoon, sensing that here were people who didn't let you go easily. Each time the parrot finished a croquette, it rattled the cage door with its beak until it was handed another.

Mme Loison and the parrot carried this on for some time. They all looked at the estate agent for approval. He felt stifled. The air was full of the smell of fried food and some kind of hair spray or cheap perfume. The whole place was overheated.

After a while, they pulled themselves together and showed him round the house.

Loison showed him the thermostats he'd installed in every room. In case the heating might fall below 30°C, thought the estate agent. Throughout the house, the decor was dark as the grave, and they stumbled from one floor to the other on steep, ill-lit stairs. Loison had also dragged bags of cement all the way to the top and built a roof terrace, only it had no view and you had to climb a ladder to get to it.

'The *marinas* is on its way,' said Loison.

This was a sea wind that would make things even damper. When it came from the east it was called *Le Grec*, as if it had blown all the way from Greece.

'I'm from Paris,' Mme Loison told him as they climbed back down, in a voice that said he should have recognized the accent that made her different from the locals.

He could see it now: a hairdressing salon or a rooms-by-the-hour hotel in rue St. Denis. Right enough, the bedrooms here wore as much wallpaper as any cheap Parisian hotel. Wooden beams had been plastered first then wallpapered. The interior of each bedroom door was also carefully wallpapered.

Mme Loison emphasized where each light switch was, in a way that suggested the estate agent would be showing people around next time. Then she dropped out and left them to visit the cellar together without her: '*entre hommes*,' as she put it. Between men.

Mr Loison led the way down the stone stairs and they arrived in a tall space built into the rock. The door directly onto the street was where they used to bring the grapes in and the wine out, Loison explained unnecessarily. There was a toilet too, which meant he could come down here any time and stay as long as he liked.

Loison shot the lights on suddenly and the estate agent saw it: on a huge purpose-built platform, a fully electrified train set had been installed among carefully-built mountains and hills. In defiance of any precise geographical location, Loison's handyman landscape contained city roads, country roads, town houses and country houses.

The estate agent could see why Mme Loison stayed away: this dungeon was her husband's *pièce de résistance*, his other world, his own peculiar damp-smelling freedom.

Loison studied the estate agent for reactions. Seeing none, he threw another switch and lights winked all over the scene. They both gazed in silence for a moment, and the estate agent almost jumped when Loison finally set the train into motion.

Lamps glowed through the windows of houses built on escarpments of Japanese wallpaper, torches glowed in the hills, while in the town traffic lights blinked, street lights swayed and bells rang as that wonderful train went by.

They both stared.

Loison looked at the estate agent and waited.

The estate agent could not find a suitable thing to say, indeed it seemed as if a word would choke him. All he could do was watch the performance.

Suddenly Loison tripped the switch and the show was over. 'I come from here but I met her when I worked in Paris,' he said. 'It's hard, a summer place, when summer is gone.' He didn't seem to expect a reply.

Slowly the two men made their way upstairs again.

The estate agent filled out the last formalities on his standard agency form at the kitchen table.

The parrot dozed.

When the estate agent came to the standard question— Reason for selling?—he couldn't bring himself to ask, and left the space blank.

As he walked back up the narrow street, he felt he had in some way failed the clients. Worse than that, he had somehow failed himself.

It's Not About the Money

Chantal had a voice like a drag queen, and one of those blonde bouffant hairstyles that went with it. A baroque version of what was once known as a French pleat, I believe.

She came to us on some kind of transfer scheme. It was that or get pre-retired, and at her age she couldn't afford that, any more than anyone else. At the interview (it wasn't an interview, she'd been parachuted in over his head) our boss told her she wasn't bad looking at all. Already nervous, she nearly jumped a yard off the ground when he then asked her if she'd ever been through analysis.

'Oh, là-là!' she said, in that double-pitch of hers, when she came out to the coffee corner. She was in a bit of a state, but braving it out.

I did my best to reassure her: he was like that, he said the same to everybody, he was bull-goose loony. We called him Madame behind his back. We asked each other, 'How's *she* doin' today?' when we wanted to know what mood he was in. We could do it in front of him without his knowing who we were talking about. The difficulty was not to crack up with laughter.

Chantal raised her plastic cup of hot sugared and lemoned water that pretended to be tea.

'Here's lookin' at you,' she said.

Chantal joined my office, where there wouldn't have been enough of us if they'd sent in ten Chantals. Ours was one of the less obscure offices of the Préfecture de Police in Paris, charged with filtering endless streams of stressed-out, nervous immigrants. Most had insufficient documentation. If they produced all the paperwork, we found another document that was needed and managed to keep them coming back and back until an earlier in-date document was now out of date and so they had to start again. Of course there were also the over-confident ones who leaped out of flash, double-parked cars, jumped the queue and tried to pull the wool over our eyes. Sometimes they sent an envoy to do it. Sometimes it even worked. But generally the wannabe immigrants were in the asking position, we had all the power. You became immune to the misery of it all, after a while.

Chantal, a spinster farmer's daughter from a forgotten corner of Normandy, brought it all to the surface again:

'What's the cattle-crush out front, for?' she asked me that first day, during the lunch break.

She was referring to the steel barriers, erected every morning by our 'bouncers'—doormen and security men—to keep the wannabe immigrants in line.

Even I had a sense of shame, as I replied, 'Hail, rain or shine.'

'May the Lord look down on them,' said Chantal. We were unused to hearing anyone make that kind of remark these days.

'That's not all,' I explained. 'They start queuing at two o'clock in the morning because we only handle so many each day. They relay each other for toilets and coffee.'

'What must those busloads of foreign tourists—what must *the world*—think of us?'

Chantal first started seeing the shrink because she was being harassed by our boss. Either she was particularly raw-skinned, or the rest of us had just turned into the fat cows he accused us of being. It was well known that he referred to our office sniggeringly as the '*gynecea.*' From the Greek. 'Fat cows!' he would say, under his breath. 'Whores!' When angry with one of us, his favorite question to her was 'Got your period today?'

Some months after she came, Chantal started seeing a shrink once a week. Because she didn't fully believe in the shrink, really, she also read, on the side, any books of psychology she could get her hands on, or understand, as a kind of double check. In one of the books she came across an anal-hoarding sadist. It was demonstrated that Himmler and Hitler had been such individuals. Chantal said it described our boss perfectly.

We all liked it, so the name stuck.

Work was his god, the office his church. He insisted that everything be done exactly as it always had in the past. We weren't even allowed to move a desk or a chair or a plant. Every morning he whipped the bouncers downstairs into a frenzy of viciousness (he had a different method of needling men that I needn't go into here) then he came up the stairs and started on his *gynecea.*

Apart from him, our office was woman-only. An accident, they pretended. However, the bigger office in the city center—where more important things were done, like stamping a residence permit because a decision had been made elsewhere and transmitted—was mostly full of men. Me and my colleagues had long since given up wondering

104

about all that. They only gave us women the vote in 1945, for God's sake

Each morning he came up the stairs and goaded us to speed up. Every day it was something different: the queue was around the block already, the Préfet was coming on a visit, the traffic police were getting antsy, a row had broken out about placement in the queue. Whatever it was, it was our fault.

After six months of this, Chantal announced she was giving up the shrink. I asked why.

'Said I was maybe giving off the wrong signals.'

'Wouldn't believe you, huh?'

'If what I said was true, then it was so outlandish that I must be encouraging such torture.'

'What'd you do?'

'I unpacked myself from his over-comfortable chair. I stood up. I said, "How much do I owe you?"'

Shortly afterwards, one Friday in May, Chantal was due to go on holiday leave.

As if he were jealous of her time off, or angry that his favorite boxing-bag was escaping, the anal-hoarder gave her a terrible grueling that morning.

She seemed to be taking it, except that by eleven o'clock she got into a row with a wannabe. This was unusual for Chantal, and she should have known better—it was a European wannabe: white, articulate. The anal-hoarder was prowling behind her. She exploded.

'Paris is full of immigrants—full! Bad hotels are overflowing with them! The hotels are so shitty they frequently burn! We have so many immigrants we burn them alive!'

The black and brown wannabes shied back, startled yet slightly amused.

The white wannabe stalked out, threatening letters.

The anal-hoarding sadist told Chantal to go to the doctor, the chemist, anywhere only get out.

She went next door and was given a tranquilizing injection. She came back after lunch determined to finish out her day and go on holidays, 'Like an ordinary Christian,' as she said to me. She looked strained. Her French pleat was mussed, something I'd never seen before.

I put her on a back desk.

When he saw her not only back but at an unaccustomed desk, he barked, 'Either you're well enough to work or you're ill. Get on the front desk.'

This was the hot seat. People he considered particularly slow, 'having their periods' etc. were put here and personally supervised. This made everyone nervous, and provided a particularly effective wannabe filter.

Chantal seemed to be standing it quite well, considering. After lunch, the anal-hoarder stuck to his office.

Then at three o'clock or so, the computers froze, and all hell broke loose.

Chantal was assailed by people desperate to get their paperwork before the weekend. An Italian couple were getting married. A German woman had an acting role to start immediately, without her the play couldn't go on. An ailing Serb lady needed her daughter to help her in and out of hospital. And that was just the Europeans.

The anal-hoarder came out from the back like a king to his

court, studiously straightening up the cord railing that kept the upstairs rabble in line.

'What's going on?'

She explained.

'Take a look at yourself,' he said to her. 'You're ageing, fast.'

This was his tack for those he considered past their periods.

Chantal suddenly swung into action. She dived into her handbag and came out with a chemist's paper bag of medication which she waved at the wannabes.

'The whole country's on tranquillizers,' she said. 'You could do with them too,' she turned to him, 'although you might be in need of something stronger. Strait-jacketing, maybe.'

She turned to the wannabes again. 'It's a wonder any self-respecting foreigner would want hand, act or part of such a country.'

We all grinned. This was the truth. But it was all the anal-hoarding sadist needed.

'You're suspended,' he said. 'Out. Now.'

Chantal's lower lip was trembling as she grabbed her stuff and left.

She was pre-retired with less pension than she would've got, but she was delighted not to have to look at him ever again.

She decided to leave the city altogether. 'I'm baling out. They say you're only free when the kids have finished university, and the dog is dead,' she smiled. 'You could say that's about where I am, now.'

She headed for Normandy and had a look at various heaps, eventually settling on one. She came back to Paris and sold her small studio for a modest sum— 'It's a helluva lot more than I put into it,' she said.

I helped her load the hired van and we drove out to Normandy during the full fury of the sixtieth commemoration of the Allied landings.

It was not a good idea. Roads were blocked and deviated and security was at its most tense, as heads of state from far and wide made their way to Omaha Beach and the rest of it.

'Did you time this deliberately?' I asked her.

'Was so busy packing boxes I never even noticed.'

We got closer to her chosen place, and deeper and deeper into a forgotten country of little stone villages and small fields and wild hedgerows and farmyards of hens and geese and ponds of ducks. It all looked as if it hadn't changed for several centuries.

When we finally juddered up the last narrow little path— you could hardly call it a road—I was shocked.

The place was in ruins. It was a collection of stone buildings arranged in a U around a yard. The side she planned to restore first consisted of a little house attached to a barn. Both had a very deep roof, covered in artistically rusting corrugated sheets. The rest had no roof at all. Oh, it was picturesque, all right. But it was a disaster.

She showed me round, knowledgeably. Off to one side was an old mill, and a reed-ridden field that even I knew in winter would be water-sodden.

We unloaded and dispersed her stuff in places we thought waterproof. She set up tent hastily, before nightfall.

I almost felt guilty, leaving her there in the middle of nowhere, on her own.

'Go on. I'm a country girl at heart,' she said.

And I drove the van back to Paris and my job with the wannabes.

With one thing and another I didn't get out there again for months. I hired a car and drove out in boiling heat one August day, the car loaded with city goodies for Chantal. In the left lane, look-at-me sports vehicles sped past, headed for Deauville.

When I left the traffic behind and got to her place, I had time to take in the whole place again. It hadn't changed a whit. The tent was still under a lean-to. However, I glimpsed two caravans.

An elderly lady in waist-length grey hair came out of a barn towards me, walking on crutches.

When she started to speak the voice was the falsetto of Chantal. You'd have heard her three fields away. 'Oh, là-là!' she said. 'Have I been having a time of it!'

She was gabbling so much I stopped listening and just looked. Gone the French pleat. The hair was only yellow at the bottom now. She was wearing stained tracksuit bottoms and a tank top. Her face was brown, her face wrinkled without its smoothing make-up. But she looked more youthful, even happy.

She'd been collecting plums for the visiting architect and

fallen from the tree breaking several ribs.

'Without the neighbors I'd have been jiggered,' she said.

She showed me around. She'd bought a beat up old white van. There was a caravan under a hayloft and another in the house itself. One served as kitchen and the other as bedroom. There were umpteen cats, two dusty appaloosa ponies, and a donkey. The appaloosas whinnied whenever we were in earshot. 'I can't resist giving them treats,' she admitted. In another meadow two huge drays raised their heads and lumbered towards us, curiously.

'Guy couldn't feed them, nobody wanted to buy them. He was contemplating selling them to the factory for meat. So I couldn't resist.'

'And the donkey?'

'My favorite. Everyone has a donkey here,' she said. 'They keep the grass down.' She had a number of hectares, some of them rented.

Her hands were still black from picking blackberries the day before. Blackberries weren't good this year, she said, because of the drought. She had invited some people around for dinner to meet me, and was planning a barbecue. 'Although I don't usually eat meat,' she added.

She even had a garden. She was soaking nettles in water to use against unwelcome insects. Tall bluegreen absinthe plants leaned against the wind, and were intended for the same purpose.

The evening was pleasant, bucolic. The sun sank red behind Chantal's ruins as we drank *cidre bouché* and gnawed on bones. There was talk of the price of firewood (hot on the heels of gas and oil), the profitability of growing cereals (fifty hectares didn't produce sufficient revenue for a family). Maize needed prodigious amounts of water just to produce one kilo. Things like that.

This gave me time to study Chantal's guests. Most were wily-eyed peasants with rough hands and plump wives. The older ones talked of the war, as if this were expected of them. One old lady had thrown a broom at a German soldier who came looking for milk and butter. '*Nichts lait, nichts beurre*,' she had told him.

When at one point the question of our work came up, we both sighed and told them a little about our boss. We said he was a *connard*. The old lady with no fear of Germans said he sounded like a right *peau de hareng*: a right old herring-skin. We got a great laugh out of that.

One member of the company was different. For one thing, he wasn't a local at all, but where he came from was a bit vague. I never got his name right, either. There was a double name and then a nickname like Mimi or something. He sat across from me. He had dark lumpy skin and wore a leather tie with a turquoise stone in it. His greasy hair was held in a ponytail by another leather tie and turquoise stone. He smoked rollups. He appeared to be on the dole. He did odd-jobs. He sculpted with stuff he found on rubbish tips. Had I seen the horse he'd made for Chantal? I recalled a rusted effort inside one of the barns. I'd seen guys like this all over the Mediterranean.

When it was all over, people helpfully washed dishes and left them to dry on one of the various oilcloth-covered tables Chantal had laid out over the yard. I was surprised to see Ponytail stay behind when the others left. He didn't have a car either, apparently.

Chantal showed me to my quarters in the bedroom caravan, told me where best to pee and how to block the door against cats, grass-snakes, foxes—

'Stop! I said. 'I'll be wanting back to my seventeen square meters, if you tell me any more!'

Then she and Ponytail retired to the tent on the sheltered side of the house.

I lay awake for a long time thinking about all that.

In the morning, Ponytail had to have hot chocolate, while we had coffee from big heavy bowls. He wasn't after the calcium for his teeth, I reckoned, because one or two were already missing. Others looked ready to follow.

It was hot. Chantal had no electricity yet, and flies came and went and laid eggs in any dead meat left lying. The cats deposited dead mice or else came with live ones and consumed them whole before our eyes—tails, teeth, and all. We walked lots. Around the locality, Parisians repaired their roofs, clipped their hedges and generally prepared to batten down the hatches for winter. 'You'd wonder,' said Chantal, 'what amusement they get out of their holidays at all.'

Ponytail said he drank pastis in the evenings. I discovered he drank it at any time of day, forcing it on anyone who dropped in to see Chantal. Sometimes he even bought a bottle from the travelling grocer, in case he'd run short.

One evening, he took us to a bar he liked to frequent— what he called a 'decent drinkers' bar'—in a nearby village. 'Le Novelty' it was called. There was a giant union jack on the back wall. It was a favorite haunt for tourist Brits.

Luckily for us the Brits weren't there that day. But Ponytail could talk of little else, and the bartender was equally enthusiastic. He looked at Chantal, and said, 'I hear the table groans with food over in your place.' He gave the impression that his bar specialized in English-speakers. 'There's X from Scotland,' he said, 'and Y from Wales, and—'

Suddenly a local man at one of the tables spoke up:

'A bird in the hand is worth two in the bush,' he announced. 'I'm sitting here and no one to even ask if I have a drought on me.'

On the fifteenth of August in the village there was a huge fete to commemorate the war. Film of elderly people recounting their war was followed by folk dancing and storytelling—much of it extremely lewd. Then a sound-and-light show at the old chateau recounted how village and chateau had been torched by the Germans on the eve of their departure. *On this very day, sixty years ago.* I'd seen various rehearsals in Paris, with jeeps and men in uniform, but somehow all this brought it closer to home. Here, the noise and dust were more real. The show ended with the arrival of a fleet of old American vehicles belching black fumes and teeming with young people, the women in light frocks and ankle socks, the men in army uniforms. All smoked cigarettes and tapped hands and feet to Glen Miller. This was followed by fireworks as good as any in Paris. We *oohed* and we *aahed* and made our way home on foot, with cricks in our necks.

I got into the habit of going out to visit Chantal often. I suppose I envied her in a way.

Ponytail was more often absent than present, especially when I came. He was very friendly with the son of a British couple who owned a manor house in the region, an idle young man in his early twenties whom I earmarked straight away for a junkie ('God silence your viper tongue!' said Chantal.) Ponytail was helping the Brits with work on their house, he was sculpting for them. The parents were rich early-retired. Their main activity was studying the French. 'They're always whining,' Ponytail informed us. It wasn't a complaint, he was studying them studying us. 'When she goes shopping, she complains that the French're either over-eager to do the hard sell or they just ignore you while they concentrate on stylish layout. It could be tomatoes or designer goods—doesn't matter.'

It had taken the Brits several years to come up with their big theory about the French: *It's not about the money*. The French were sex and food addicts, hedonists if you wanted to be polite about it. They were terribly focused on remaining secular. They were frequently revolting. They were always arrogant. But throughout all of that you had to hand it to them, because while the rest of the world was hell bent on getting rich or being rich, the French still preferred to talk about 'decent' wages and quality of life. *It wasn't about the money*.

Chantal and I stuck to our more earthly pursuits. Her house had clearly become a sort of halfway house where all dropped in and many stayed to eat. I never saw anyone bring her anything, but imagined there must be some arrangement between them. A man came and pared the donkey's hooves. Four rounds of dark nail, with a half-moon of paler substance, sat on the flagstones before the house. The locals sat and watched and said nothing. I learned about aphids and compost and that anything you planted on the feast of Sainte Catherine would grow.

When I was there, I wished I was back in Paris, and when I was back in Paris I could think of nothing better than being out in the country again.

We went mushrooming in autumn, as work began on Chantal's roof. This was a huge affair, and I didn't dare ask how much it was costing or if she'd have anything left over. Ponytail was spending more and more time with the Brits. That way he avoided getting involved in any of the work on the house. They'd lodged him in an empty wing of the house. But occasionally he graced us with his presence and came smelling of pastis and rollups. He told us about the arguments he'd had with the Brits over William the Conqueror. 'They think they invaded France!' he chortled. The young man, his new friend, was called William, which led to further chortling. Ponytail had done his homework: 60 percent of the English language came from either Norman or French—and they weren't the same thing, he reminded us. Nobody, not even the Allies, had managed to bomb the Conqueror's chateaux to bits. The Conqueror had built the Tower of London. The Normans had gone on the Crusades. There were people with names of Norman origin in Sicily and the Middle East.

And so on, and so on.

After the roof, Chantal attacked the house itself. She had the walls sanded to bring out the stone, and this is where she got a big surprise. One day the workmen came running to say there was a 'problem': they'd have to stop sanding in order to strip a wall that seemed to be covered in tons of plaster. 'Could be anything under there—maybe the wall's in trouble,' they said helpfully. The wall was seriously bulbous.

I wondered why the architect hadn't gone into the question, but kept my mouth shut.

Chantal wanted everything out in the open and upfront. 'Let's strip it and know the worst,' she said.

So they went through layers of plaster until they came to stone. It took ages. I was there for the start of it, but then I had to leave again.

'Anyone that hasn't got a layer of fat on them now, is fucked,' a customer remarked to the cheese vendor as I hovered in the market one early winter day. I was waiting for Chantal to collect me. I had abandoned cars for the leisurely train.

A bitter wind blew through the cheese vendor's hair. She checked her clients for offence-caliber, and giggled.

When we got to the house, I was astonished. Inside the main living room was a chimney the size of the entire wall. The stone was beautiful. The corbels were sculpted.

'Why on earth would anyone want to hide that?' I asked.

'Nobody knows anything,' she said. 'I've checked high and low. You'd be forgiven for feeling paranoid.'

She had other problems too: the new phone number she'd been given turned out to be a former fax, and she kept receiving faxes during the night from advertising computers to which she couldn't reply.

'It's Kafkaesque,' she said. 'I have to unplug the phone to

sleep. But if I forget, I'm done for.'

Telecom refused to help; all they could do was change her number again.

There was also trouble about a septic tank she'd had installed by a local, without taking account of the new European rules and regulations and permissions and technical considerations.

To cap it all, the next-door farmer was after her land.

'Sometimes,' she eyed me carefully as she said it, 'I think there's a jinx on me.'

It got so bad that I worried for her, and having little else to do, I went out there for Christmas. We chose pigments, and painted wall after wall. Then we sat before the huge chimney and with giant tongs fiddled with logs a yard long in the great fire. I had to admit Chantal had made a great job of the huge room with its high-beamed ceiling. She hadn't gone too precious on it, but had left a certain rusticity, all the better to set off the antiques she was collecting all over the region. She'd even got good at beating Parisian dealers to the choicest items. After Christmas we continued 'the hunt' as she referred to it. On good days, she'd say, 'Bagged plenty,' on bad days, 'Nothing bagged.'

It even snowed and the electricity blacked out. We spent a whole evening by candlelight, eating food produced on the fire. Chantal was in her element. She had found catechism benches somewhere and cleaned them up for the kitchen table. As we sat there with friends or neighbors, she'd suddenly say, 'Who made the world?,' then answer herself, 'God made the world.' Then, 'Who do we call God?' Even

117

the locals didn't remember such basics. Some of it contrasted oddly with the antiques and the rest.

It all contrasted utterly with our poor wannabes I'd left behind in the heart of the city.

The following summer, Chantal came to Paris more often. She came for specific events like the Fête de la Musique on the longest day, and later she came again for the fourteenth of July. I wondered what it all meant. I found out that Ponytail was looking after the garden and the animals in her absence. 'I didn't leave him a key,' she added, 'he has no business inside the house and there's the insurance to think of. Anyway, I'm paying him for it, he's strapped at the moment.'

In August we went back to Normandy together and found things a mess. The garden was parched and yellow. More dramatically, even the animals were dry. Nobody had seen Ponytail for days. A neighbor had only noticed the situation hours before, but had done little other than water the animals.

'I need to have this out with him,' she said.

Inside the house, there was a dreadful smell. She seemed more worried about Ponytail than the smell.

'Must be the septic tank,' she said lightly. 'I'll put a dose of 'Urgent' in it.'

Because we hadn't found out where Ponytail had gone and because I'd always wanted to see it, I dragged her next morning—protesting—off to a local hunting fete, where horses, dogs and men were blessed from the altar and long polished horns were sounded during Mass. Something else struck me too: here was another, utterly non-peasant side of local life. Pedigree dogs and horses were not only pure-bred but impeccably groomed with shiny backsides and evenly-trimmed tails, unlike the dusty appaloosas in Chantal's back field. The men and women mounted on them were beefy, well-fed and sleek, in utter contrast to the specimens that frequented Chantal's place. Their gear was their best, for the festival, green outfits and black outfits and grey and stunning red with matching hats, feathers and sometimes a white fur trim. They walked and talked with the confidence of people who were afraid of nothing and owed nothing to anyone, the kind who could train or whip a horse or a dog and buy or sell a bishop or a gendarme. It was a whole side of local life I knew nothing about, and that Chantal chose to ignore.

We wandered and talked throughout the day, but I couldn't distract her from the problem of the missing Ponytail.

Finally we decided to brazen it out, go over to the Brits' house and ask for him. As we left the hunting festival we stumbled on a mountain of backed-up traffic. We were forced to make a huge deviation. The gendarmes directing the heavy traffic were polite but unrelenting: you kept moving and you went where they told you. That was all.

'I wouldn't have the courage if you weren't with me,' Chantal said. 'Anyway, the longer we stay away from home, the better chance the smell will be gone.'

So we rattled over there and up their avenue in the yellowing van.

Here was utter contrast to Chantal's abode. Lawns and flowerbeds had been landscaped, then neatly manicured. Windows shone.

'Not a hair out of place,' said Chantal.

The doors and shutters were a Laura Ashley green.

'Very British,' I said.

The Brits, it turned out, weren't interested in her problem.

'Our son William has gone missing,' they said, in their impeccable lounge. There seemed to be something else, but they didn't want to talk to us. Ponytail seemed much less important than a son.

Chantal was silent as we drove back to her place.

'What do you make of all this?' she said finally.

I couldn't help her, didn't know how deep she was in, but it was clear that she thought Ponytail must be involved with the Brit's disappearance somehow.

After a day of agonizing and doing everything in our power to reduce the smell, which seemed to have settled in the kitchen of all places, we went to the gendarmes.

They questioned Chantal for a while, then sent us into another office. A higher-up gendarme came in, removed his kepi from a sweating forehead, and said,

'The news is bad, I'm afraid. Car accident.' He watched us for reactions. 'Mr Grigoriou was killed instantly. 'About an hour from your place.'

Ponytail had had his last pastis and hot chocolate. They hadn't contacted Chantal because she wasn't family. In fact, it had taken them a while to track down his family. He seemed to be out of contact with them. They turned out to be in the middle of Paris. I asked him to repeat the family name.

'Greek,' said the gendarme. 'Greek, from Barbès.'

I was briefly reminded of our wannabes.

By now the entire house was pervaded with the awful smell. It had seeped into all the rooms, attached itself to the upholstery. Even when we showered, it seemed to remain on our skin.

I dug out sleeping tablets for her and for me.

After a fitful night I got Chantal out of there as best I could. I arranged for the farmer neighbor to look after the animals and the mail, and took her back to Paris with me. The problem of smells and septic tanks I left for another day.

She actually made me go with her to Ponytail's funeral. I don't know what we expected, but there wasn't a funeral as such. They'd had him incinerated. In a small whitewashed courtyard in Barbès—not unlike how I imagined Greece—his ashes sat on a windowsill in a grey plastic urn. A sad and motionless black-clad mother sat on a wooden chair, surrounded by a huge extended family. They were having a *mechoui*, more to feed the multitude than to celebrate anything, least of all Ponytail's passing.

We were received and entertained by an older brother of Ponytail. He had organized everything. 'For the mother, mostly,' he said. Of the adults of our own age, he was the only one who spoke to us in French. No one talked of Ponytail. The brother talked of his own retirement, slated for six months' time. He would go to Greece, where with a tomato and a piece of bread you could feed yourself. 'Hope she lives long enough for me to take her back,' he indicated the silent mother. A Greek was not like a Frenchman. 'If you're hungry,' he said, 'another Greek will feed you. There's solidarity over there, there's none in France.' He was a member of one of the redder trade unions. He'd been working in Renault when the riots broke out in '68. The riot police wouldn't go in there: 'The CRS didn't dare.' The first thing he'd do if he were Prime Minister of France, would be to close down all these charitable organizations and give everyone a room and access to sanitary facilities. 'We don't want charity,' he said, 'we want treating like human beings.' Their own house—a collection of small houses surrounding the yard—had started life as a squat. Little by little, the family had grown and invested the abandoned shells. No one knew who owned them. The town hall had to do something about housing people. They were helping them with the paperwork to purchase it.

It all seemed to bring some peace to Chantal. She stayed in the city for ages, even met up with Ponytail's older brother occasionally for chats in cafes about the way the world was going. She was amazed that she could like the city again, in love with city life as for the first time, astonished to see how swollen the immigrant population had become. When she said, with a wry smile, 'You people not doing your job?' I knew it was time to talk to her about going back.

I took a late-autumn week, with the anal-hoarding sadist's approval.

We trained it out there. The van was still rusting in the station lot where we'd left it. We had to get a garage to jump-start it.

The house looked abandoned, but the animals were glad to see us.

Inside, the smell was still there, but fainter. We threw open the windows.

'The bloody tank, I suppose,' said Chantal. 'I'll put a dose in it.'

The house was chill too.

'I'm going to light the fire,' Chantal announced. 'That's what I missed most in Paris.'

The fire was difficult to get going. 'Chimney's good and cold,' Chantal said, working away at it like a professional. 'Always like this, the first fire of the winter.'

The smoke began to fill the room. She still didn't panic. 'That's funny,' she said, 'it's never done that before.'

She opened the door. 'Create a draft,' she said. 'I forgot to have the chimney cleaned this summer.'

Even when there was a rustling noise in the chimney she still didn't panic.

'I've even had birds and their nests falling into it.'

Then it happened.

A foot fell into the fireplace.

We shot to our feet and recoiled. We recognized it as a foot because there was a shoe, and even a sock, but the bones and the rest of it only became clear after a lot of 'Oh, là-là!' and dragging it out of the embers with the mercifully long tongs.

Then of course a foot begged the question of a body.

And sure enough, when we got the courage to look, the rest of the body was still up there. Stuck, so to speak, between heaven and hell. Chantal blessed herself and went to the phone.

It took some persuading. No one would believe her.

She pressed the loudspeaker button. 'You pulling my wire?' a policeman asked. 'The other one has bells on it.'

Chantal was somewhere between laughing and crying. I took the phone and explained. As I hung up, it struck me that maybe her ambiguous falsetto didn't help.

When coroner, gendarmes, firemen and all the others who eventually turned up had done with us and 'it,' and had taken 'it' away, Chantal poured us both a stiff glass of *goutte*.

'It was the Brit,' she said, huddling up to an electric radiator.

'What?'

I thought she might be losing it again, like the day the computers crashed.

'It was William, Mimi's friend.'

We both studied the now-empty fireplace.

'They're expecting me in town tomorrow. To fill out a report.'

She was still amazingly calm.

'They reckon he came to burgle the house,' she said quietly.

I burst out laughing. 'With all the dosh they have, and the Laura Ashley paint?'

'Not the parents, the son. The gendarmes said burglary was quite common in unoccupied country houses.'

'There you are!' I said, overenthusiastically. 'Yours is occupied!'

Next day, we went to the gendarmerie.

One unoccupied night is enough, they told her. The British boy, as they called him, would have needed the money for drugs. The antiques were always saleable, no questions asked. Paris dealers were always interested.

They'd examined his mobile phone messages. He'd got stuck in the chimney. He'd phoned Ponytail for help. They surmised that Ponytail had hightailed it off to get help from someone like himself, but unused to the car, and preoccupied, he'd gone straight through a dangerous crossroads. Nobody suggested he was running.

What shocked me most was what Chantal said next:

'I keep imagining William there in the chimney, waiting for Mimi to come back. I think of his dawning realization that Mimi has betrayed him. Just imagine his thirst, the fatigue, the hunger, the thirst, the terrible need for the drug...'

I took her out of there. Again.

I helped her sell the place—the price was rock-bottom after all that had happened and the greedy farmer got it for a song, horses and all. I arranged for her to sign it all in a Paris notary's office. Before that I went out there and got a dealer she knew to take the antiques. He was keeping them in a warehouse until Chantal decided what she wanted to do.

'Let it go,' said Chantal when it was done, as if I were the one selling. 'Like I let go the anal-hoarding sadist, and Mimi and a whole host of stuff.'

She never talked about young William in the chimney anymore, but she started going into churches more often, lighting candles. Things like that.

125

Back in the office that winter, old Herringskin, as our boss was now known, became unbearable. He was pushing more of our buttons than ever before, pushing everyone equally. You'd be forgiven for thinking he missed Chantal.

At my instigation, we struck. We got out and demonstrated on the street with the wannabes. He tried to fire more of us for incompetence, but it was too late. We sued for harassment. Chantal came in with us. We all got a small stipend.

But it wasn't about the money. We were happier at last and free at last and Chantal's voice came down an octave and we could look at ourselves in the mirror again.

I SAY 'GOOD MORNING' TO MY TRUCK

The evening I met him I had just run out of the house because of a strange and disturbing impression.

It was Sunday night, post-dinner you could say. I eat sporadically and when really hungry I go up to Les Platanes, a bar-restaurant with a comfy ageing blonde manager and food you'd die for. The *Changement de Propriétaire* sign has been draped across the front for years. The interior décor was obviously once designed for a Chinese place, all red flocking and whorls. This is confused with some North African objects, by way of a statement, I suppose, or else in search of a clear sign that isn't Chinese.

But to get back to me for a minute. Although it was a winter's evening, I still had all the curtains open. I like to do that because, paradoxically, it deters the nosy-parker across the yard, who spends her time hanging out the window chain-smoking. I like to catch the last of the sun reflected in the windows opposite (I face east, it's cheaper), and spot individual lights as they come on, and finally to appreciate the fully-lit ensemble of the other buildings around. I fantasize about occupants of those rooms that peek around the corner of our yard, rooms whose shutters stay closed for days on end, then open to expose the cheap ceiling chandelier in all its glory, while three sets of men's laundry are clumsily and hastily festooned around the window to dry.

Since we're on the edge of the city, some of these hotels serve as coach-stages for happy families on their way to Euro Disney, but others tell a different tale, are called *"meublés"* and house people down on their luck whose rent is paid by social services because they can't pay the now exorbitant Paris rents.

So there I was, seated at my table—a big table for someone who never eats at home—drinking something, and flicking through a magazine. In the big mirror—big to give the illusion of space, create an Alice-in-Wonderland other room I can never reach –I suddenly caught sight of a high-rise block through the window, and across the gardens, behind me.

It caught my eye because it seemed to have moved *nearer*. In fact it seemed to me, for a moment, that it was approaching our building at a fair speed.

Get a grip, I muttered to myself. Without verification or reflection, I grabbed my coat and headed out to the street, skipping down the stairs without even waiting for the lift.

Outside it was colder than I expected, with a searing wind. Few people were abroad. I remembered hearing a weather forecast about snow on low ground, expected avalanches, traffic bottlenecked, ski resorts full to bursting.

The usual pre-spring scene.

I headed for Les Platanes. The usual fug of warmth, good food and drink greeted me. The habitual hangers-on were around the bar, with a few new faces from the hotels round about. The talk batted around this and that, politics and habits, with the occasional guffaw or sneer from us or the man behind the bar, who seemed to have no end of glasses

128

to dry. Maybe it's an obsessive-compulsive thing with him. The ageing blonde came and went from the restaurant tables, mothering late customers—mostly single men from the hotels roundabout—and smiling a homely smile. Some of the men at the bar had plastic bags of shopping at their feet, baguettes peeking. That meant they'd perhaps been there since the Sunday morning market on the canal. Nobody seemed drunk or disorderly. I always reckoned this was due to the presence of the motherly blonde.

There comes a moment, in Les Platanes, when you know it's time to go. The glass-drier behind the bar and the blonde never actually say anything, you just begin to feel uncomfortable. It's related to some unseen control that keeps everyone from getting drunk and shouting and becoming aggressive. You know it really is time to call it a day when the Algerian—yes, the sublime French food is cooked by a North African—finally slinks out of the kitchen and slides towards the door, as if trying for invisibility.

This is the moment when I pay up and go, for I can't be bothered having my last drink ruined by some unseen, unbidden haste.

I scrunched my shoulders and collar up, headed out into the now sub-zero temperature for what I call home. Ahead of me, equally hunched, was a small dark man carrying a plastic bag of shopping. As I levelled with him he looked up, and I recognized him as one of the men from the bar, men I normally consider to be just numbers, ships that pass in the night.

I said, 'Good Evening,' recalling, as I did so, a phrase of my father's: *Whiskey talks.*

The little man smiled and moved into step with me, and I wondered if greeting him hadn't been a bad idea.

'Back to work tomorrow, *hein?*' he grinned. 'Actually, I never do anything else only work. When one job is finished, the boss calls me on the mobile and away I go again. Never see home. I have a *meublé* here and another in Cherbourg.' His attachment to his rented rooms—he made them sound like Riviera properties—reminded me of student bedsits in northern cities, of men who came to collect rent late on Friday nights, counting the cash slowly and entering it in a notebook, each room with a rat in a trap sitting on his bed, waiting for the man to knock.

'Not that home is any great shakes either,' he said. 'I come from St Georges de Bagnoles, a miserable place—two houses and a church.'

He paused. I hoped he wasn't going to cry or something.

'Trucking is a strange existence. You have no friends, no family.' This didn't seem to upset him unduly. 'Ended up in all kinds of trouble.'

I thought of the influence of the homely blonde. I wondered how much drink he'd taken. He didn't appear drunk.

As if he had read my thoughts, he said, 'We can't drink from Monday to Friday, you know, not a solitary drop.' He scraped his thumb under his front teeth, to indicate zilch.

His baguette was taking a beating—squashed under his arm and beginning to fold in two. I couldn't help wondering what it would taste like in the morning.

His story was complex. There was a lot of it, and I didn't follow it all due to his diction.

However, somewhere in there I got hooked.

'*Tu m'énerves*,' he had said to a gendarme, way back. The common mortal didn't normally tell gendarmes they were annoying, but I imagined truckers have a longer leash than the rest of us. The gendarme hadn't got the message, had insisted on more papers and a full inspection of the truck. I'd seen these cops in their bike gear on motorways, their knee boots affirming that they wouldn't suffer fools lightly. The trucker had finally lost his patience and roughed up the gendarme, catching him by his jacket and shaking him.

He was silent for a moment.

I waited, studying his diminutive appearance, searching for the toughness I hadn't noticed before. I marveled at the hidden treasures and even major dangers to be found bottled up, standing beside one at a bar or in the street.

'Married five times,' he said.

There had been one daughter.

'Grew up without me around.'

He hadn't seen her from babyhood to womanhood. Most of the rare times he was home, she was in bed asleep.

'You're not going to waken a kid at two a.m.,' he said, 'for your own purposes.'

There also seemed to have been some major piece of bad luck, a bigger background he hadn't got to yet. He was getting stuck into his story now, and I hoped that his discourse was heading for some dénouement or other, before we froze to death in the windswept street.

We paused at a corner and faced each other. I felt like one of the wedding guests who'd run into the Ancient Mariner.

I hunted my memory for what he had already said, but

couldn't find any major thing I'd missed. The incident with the gendarme had just been a rite of passage, it seemed.

I made suitable noises. I wanted him to spit it out. My attitude seemed to encourage him.

His mother stood by him through all of it, he went on. He lived with her and turned all his money over to her, unlike his brothers. I imagined a whole family of diminutive pent-up violence. I thought of a wife, children, money trouble.

But it wasn't any of these.

Now he straightened his shoulders, as he declared, 'Shot a man stone dead. Did five years for it.'

He didn't wait to see what effect this would have, his confidence in me already assured.

'We all carry a gun, you know?'—he waited to see if I knew.

I nodded, lying, and hiding my surprise at the occasions for violence that sail blithely past us daily on roads and motorways.

'Well, we carry big sums in cash, for one thing and another. For the truck, for repairs, for petrol, for accommodation and food, for urgent cargoes, whatever.'

He wasn't even in his truck when it had happened. One night, in some provincial town or other, a chap in an anorak with the hood up had noticed him in a shop or a bar and followed him home to his *meublé*. 'If he knew I was a trucker, he knew I'd have a wad of money. I could hear his footsteps behind me. I was near the door of the hotel when I heard him come at me, fast, from behind. I was ready for him. I drew my gun, turned, and shot him dead.'

He studied my reaction. I was suitably impressed.

'Self-defense all right, that was no problem. It was what I'd done to the gendarme that complicated my case. Sent me to a shrink. A female. Screwed her as well. She was dying for it. Strictly against the rules, but mum's the word.'

I tried to imagine a shrink who'd be dying to make love to this small violent man at the risk of losing her job and career. Yet he was strangely convincing. Perhaps she'd fallen for it too. Or perhaps he really was an innocent.

He giggled.

'Then she stood up for me in court—I was upstanding, honest, all that sort of stuff. Which was true. The boy's family were all there too—the mother and all, looking for compensation. How were they to manage without him, that kind of thing.'

We hovered in front of a door, which turned out to be the hotel whose back peeked onto our yard. Single men of all colors made their way around us through the Art Nouveau doors to the cheap-chandeliered interior, grunting anonymous greetings at each other and us, a minor hold-up in an organized existence.

The bitter black wind blew up stronger from the wilds beyond the city boundaries, and I knew I'd soon have to head for home. I made a shift at taking my adieus, but he wasn't finished yet. He was getting to the important bit.

'Every morning, I have a hearty breakfast and I head for my truck. I go round it, check everything outside. Then I get in, pat the seats, look around, smell it all—'

He studied my face carefully.

'—and I say "Good Morning" to my truck.'

He started moving towards the hotel entrance.

'And I drive off, a free man,' he said, as he swept through the wrought-iron doors.

The cold wind bundled me home. Before lighting the lights I looked outside. The high-rises were not so much moving nearer as floating.

There we were, all glowing and floating, like tall ships on a night sea.

PLUGGING THE CAUSAL BREACH

When Bea and I first came to Paris, we were still so wrapped up in each other we didn't see much of our neighbor, Marie-Louise. She and a Vietnamese couple were the only other people sharing the lift with us. I did notice she was peculiar, with big fuzzy hair that was obviously dyed and glowed purplish against the light. She had a gummy smile, the rare time we saw it, but as my girlfriend Bea said, that was hardly her fault. There were times when we would meet her down on the street and she wouldn't even see us.

Marie-Louise rarely had visitors, although she had a mother in the suburbs and a sister who was married somewhere in town. Bea (who found out most of this) swears she actually met the mother once, helped carry her bag up the stairs, and found her strangely unfriendly.

'You fabulate, my dear,' I told Bea that time. 'It's the causal breach. You women are obsessed by it. Spend all your time trying to plug it, searching for reasons and explanations.'

Marie-Louise had a cat. We first got to know her when she asked us to feed the cat one time she went to a clinic to lose weight. I hated the cat, its litter, its smells. I mentioned toxoplasmosis.

'One always hates other people's cats, Frank,' Bea said.

Marie-Louise was clearly obsessed about filling the causal breach, that void between an event and its explanation, something that fascinated me too, although I didn't say so to Bea.

Marie-Louise had a selection of odd occurrences she brought up from time to time, as if requesting or hoping for an explanation. One story was the day she and her husband were travelling along somewhere in Europe in what she called 'Our Bug' (a VW beetle), on a normal bright partly-cloudy day. The countryside was hilly but the road—an old coach road—instead of going round the hills went up and down each one as it came. This was fun. You could see she was reliving the experience each time she told it.

The climax was that they topped a hill and suddenly there was a line across the road where snow began and beyond it a winter world of white, with several trucks backed up at a service station surrounded by drifts. Her husband, who was driving, got such a fright he almost skidded, and had to slow down gradually before he was able to turn and go back.

Go back? Why? Where were they headed?

She couldn't remember, and always closed up at this point.

Bea said it was a freak snowstorm, and nothing more.

Marie-Louise worked at the Post Office next door, along with what I considered to be a selection of other social cases, all swollen from a lack of exercise and the drugs they needed to regulate their serotonin. That was how I explained them to myself, although Bea just laughed. 'You're the one with the problem,' she'd say whenever I complained about their queuing system or the fact that they refused to sell me international reply coupons. 'We don't do them anymore,' they'd say firmly without even checking, and I'd have to lope off to another branch.

Marie-Louise and her husband had traveled the world: Russia, the east-bloc countries in their darkest days, southern Europe, the great outdoor spaces of the American West. She knew all the most beautiful spots, the have-to-see places in every country, although she often preferred to fix on something peculiar. Her favorite story was of the laughing clubs they'd visited in India. 'They'd start with the vowels,' she'd say; then she'd shout: 'He! Ha! Ho! Hi! Hu!' Sometimes it seemed to be the only thing they'd done or seen in India.

Those days we didn't know exactly where the husband was, although Marie-Louise never mentioned being divorced, or referred to herself as a divorcee. Eventually it emerged that his name was Vlasta and that he had come from Eastern Europe and gotten rich, a long time ago. 'Ah, Vlasta!' she would say with a despairing wave of her arm. In winter she gave Saturday theatre classes to small groups of people like herself, in an under-sized sitting room lined with cheap reproductions of old masterpieces. She pretended her family had known many of the most famous modern painters and reckoned that, as a young girl, she'd shown her bum to more than one of them. 'Small girls do that, you know,' she said. She had gone on to become their model.

At twelve years of age, she had ceremoniously binned her very ancient and much-thumbed copy of *Alice in Wonderland*, illustrated by Tenniel, with its talking sheep and sinister cats. I thought this chain of events worthy of psychoanalysis, but Bea said she was just chatting. Bea sometimes made a cake and invited Marie-Louise to share it. I would come home and find two sets of big teeth grinning over tea and cake, sharing gossip about the building and its occupants.

Marie-Louise called our *concierge* The Queen of Hearts. 'Queen of Hearts giving orders again?' she'd enquire when some directive appeared in our letterboxes. *Residents must realize... Residents should note...* The Queen of Hearts was a tiny dark Portuguese Catholic, trying to be a tall blonde one. She had a small white poodle and a huge Rottweiler (these I referred to as her Manichean aspects). She took lunch with her parents every Sunday in a public-housing block to the west of Paris which had replaced the shanty town where they lived on their arrival in 1960s France, fleeing Salazar and all that. She was convinced that some saint or other had recently saved her kid from certain death in a scooter accident. She also reckoned we were in constant danger of our lives from local hooligans—hence the Rottweiler—and had organized teams of solemn young men in what looked like Ninja-turtle outfits to patrol the yard and gardens. When the details appeared on the annual charges billed at the beginning of the year, I almost had a fit.

'Time for you to get interested in your fellow man, Frank,' Bea advised me. 'This one has been coming at us for a while.'

As a teenager Marie-Louise had been propositioned, very correctly, by a painter friend of her parents. Politely, in his car, after school. When she refused, equally politely, he drove off and she never saw him again. The thing was she had fancied him terribly and had cried when his wife died and he married a second time. 'Wanting things to stay forever in one place,' she said, 'that's kids for you.'

On Sunday afternoons in winter she sometimes went to what she called a '*Thé dansant*' in old-fashioned Paris ballrooms where tea and cakes were served and polite men asked her to dance dances you really had to know: 'You can't improvise a tango,' she'd say. She had some kind of regular dancing partner at these dancing teas, whom she called her '*Bon ami*' and whose name we never learned.

''Cos he doesn't exist,' I said.

'You should cut down on philosophy and read more fiction,' said Bea, 'they say it helps us empathize.'

Someone pinched my shoulder-bag one day in the metro when I was lost in a book. Bea wasn't home when I got there, so I knocked on Marie-Louise's door. I'd even contemplated asking our Vietnamese neighbor rather than getting involved with Marie-Louise. But I knew the Vietnamese woman would have her own story about a woman's life in Vietnam, how she only ever went out on her own to go to Mass (our neighbors are Vietnamese Catholics) and how even their watches and wedding rings were taken from them when they left Vietnam. She'd told all this to Bea, who concluded they were terrified of anyone with administrative power over them. Rather than question any authority, they paid all bills without question, including the one for the Ninja turtles.

So I knocked and explained why I needed somewhere to wait till Bea arrived. Marie-Louise ushered me into the sitting room with the reproductions. I was halfway across the dark room when I realized there was someone else there.

'Vlasta, Frank,' she said simply.

'Get a glass for Frank,' Vlasta told Marie-Louise, as if he came every day, lived there, or even owned the place.

For a while he interviewed me like a prospective husband

139

for a daughter, then settled into the story of his own life. He seemed to have a wife, although I couldn't be sure, and he certainly had two teenage sons who seemed to cause him endless hassle. I presumed he'd made them with someone other than Marie-Louise.

'Bought them a 7-11 store,' he said, 'and they're about to run it into the ground as well—they're too lazy even to sit at the till and take in the money.'

He launched into wider subjects. 'The Americans organized the Twin Towers themselves. Did you see the way they came down?' —it wasn't a question— 'The plane only hit the corner of the building. Had to have explosives planted all over it.' And the Americans didn't care, he said, because the towers were full of foreigners.

Glued to my chair in horror and fascination, all that seemed to be working was my tongue: I tried to move him on to other things, like the newly reduced Greater Serbia. 'Yugoslavia was ruled by non-Serbs, but the Serbs got the blame,' he told me. The trouble now was the Albanians. 'Import two of them Sheptar,' he said (I thought I saw Marie-Louise wince), 'and in no time you have hundreds.'

According to him Yugoslavia was made to fall apart eventually. 'Stalin was a priest before he came to power. He got rid of the soutane and attacked religion. Tito wasn't a Serb either, no one knows where he came from.'

'Wasn't the man who killed the Archduke Ferdinand a Serb?' I ventured, glancing at my watch.

'Sure, but he lived in Bosnia,' he replied. So he wasn't really a Serb either.

'If you meet a Sheptar'—Marie-Louise definitely

winced— 'on a country path, he marches towards you and you have to step off the path. Then he steps off the path too, to confront you again. Some people are always spoiling for a fight, like the man who comes up to a peaceful coffee drinker in a café and says, "Why did you fuck my wife?" Coffee drinker says, "I didn't go near your wife, what do I want to go fucking your wife for?" And the belligerent one changes tack: "What's wrong with my wife that you wouldn't want to fuck her?"'

And so on. My ears were tuned to the bump of the lift, but there was still no sign of Bea. Vlasta couldn't be stopped, now he had an audience. Marie-Louise busied herself with tea. 'Marx and Engels had excellent ideas that were meant to be introduced gradually,' Vlasta continued. 'But no, Lenin had to go and have his Revolution. Communism is a complete misnomer. It brought to power men who only knew how to herd sheep. Down they came from the mountains and found themselves addressing crowds. They didn't know the difference between Communism and Capitalism. They were told that Communism meant if a man has two chairs you take one off him and give it to someone who has none. One of these former shepherds, before a crowd and stuck for words, saw a tramp go by at the back of the crowd with a sack on his back. "A capitalist!" he cried. "There goes a capitalist! Take the sack off him and divide its contents among you!"'

Vlasta looked very pleased with himself. Marie-Louise winked at me surreptitiously.

Suddenly Vlasta glanced at a very expensive watch, leaped to his feet and said he couldn't delay, as if we'd tried to hold onto him.

When he was gone Marie-Louise opened the window and beckoned me over.

'Come and look,' she said. 'He likes me to wave goodbye.'

We waved as Vlasta got into a Mercedes that was several generations old and roared off in a cloud of black fumes. Just then Bea rounded the corner. We waved at her too.

'I must apologize for Vlasta's behavior,' Marie-Louise said. 'It is part of why we are no longer together. A lot of things about Vlasta were masked by language and culture, from the start.'

She paused.

'The original and correct word is *Shqiptar*,' she said, 'from the Albanian language. It's related to the word for speak. The word Vlasta used is extremely pejorative, like "Barbarian" once was for the Greeks, or "Welsh" for the Germans.'

I'd had enough by then and was in no mood for linguistics. I made for the door in haste, but Marie-Louise caught me by the arm:

'How can you see something in a mirror that isn't reflected in it directly?' she wanted to know.

She pointed out a rooftop opposite and then to its reflection in a mirror on her wall that lay at right angles to the window.

First I sighed. I could hear the lift. Then I went to a lot of trouble with paper and diagrams and angles and so on, but it was clear that she didn't believe me. She was convinced it was some kind of magic.

'I had a dream,' she said. 'I came into a room and saw a small man—tiny, really—dressed in bulky but shiny clothes, lying, obviously dead, on the floor near a chair. My first reflex was to reach out for it'—she definitely said 'it'— 'more for tidiness than anything else. Just then a very large speckled bird—as big as the little man, anyhow—took him by the beak and pulled him under the chair out of my reach.'

'So what've you been up to?' Bea challenged me as I burst into our apartment,

'Plugging the causal breach,' I said.

I kept it going for a while before telling her about Vlasta. Bea and I had reached that stage in our relationship where the lives of others filled a space between us that we couldn't fill ourselves.

That summer was the famous '*canicule,*' as they called it here (somehow a deadlier word than 'heatwave') during which France killed off some fifteen thousand of its old folks.

Early on, Bea and I enjoyed the weather, the city. One weekend we rolled out to watch the Queen of Hearts participate in a parade celebrating Portugal in all its aspects. I was truly astonished at the sheer numbers of them, their costumes, their faithfulness to regions and habits. There were groups from all over Paris with banners related to occupations, ways of life and regions in Portugal. All in costume, there were brides and grooms, kids, people carrying peasant farming tools, playing music, dancing.

I said, 'What, no tools for digging ditches?' I told Bea this was over-the-top folklore, a memory of the times before they all had to flee dictatorship and poverty and getting called up to fight wars in Angola and Mozambique.

The Queen of Hearts smiled and waved as she jigged by in a black and white outfit topped with a kind of lace mantilla.

When I said, 'No sign of the concierge's tools there,' Bea dragged me away.

After that we fled south—'Because they know how to deal with heat down there,' Bea said—until it became too much there too. Then on to Morocco to friends, until I tired of seeing rich people in rich houses surrounded by the poor padding about them, cleaning, cooking, trying for invisibility.

'And they wonder why they want to come to Europe,' I said.

'Don't start,' said Bea.

Then I had a summer school in Ireland, where my temper improved immediately in the more modest temperatures. Things in Ireland had never been better: you could sit on the grass, swim every day, organize a picnic, all without having a Plan B. Demand was so brisk that every garage and supermarket in the country ran out of charcoal for barbecues.

Late one night after Bea went to sleep, I stuck in my earphone and switched on the radio on my cell phone. A scratchy French station was talking about hundreds of deaths all over Paris. The funeral parlors were overflowing, they said. They were requisitioning cold storage places to accommodate the bodies, there were so many of them.

'What the hell is this?' I said, into the night.

It was all over by the time we got back. Paris had settled into a sinister post-disaster calm. I bought the papers in the station. The media were down to the usual ding-dong about who was to blame: society was at fault, there was no respect for the old. One family, abroad on holidays (I think—perhaps they were only in the south on a beach) asked the authorities if they would hold on to the grandmother's body till their holidays were over, 'She's dead, she's going noplace anyway,' they were reputed to have said.

The big heat was over. Our building would be pretty well empty, we reckoned, which was normal for late August. However, when we punched in our code and the door opened stiffly, who should we find standing in the hall but the Queen of Hearts.

'Still here?' we said.

'What with all that happened,' she said.

She had opened the glass door on the notice board and was fumbling with a black-edged handwritten sign. She held it up to us.

It announced that Marie-Louise was dead.

'Family won't do it,' she whispered.

Before I could ask why she was whispering, she hissed: 'Body's still up there.' She raised her eyes, 'They haven't even appeared once. No one to sit with the body. Think of it. No priest said the last prayers. Left it all to the undertakers,' she concluded, folding her arms and studying us for reactions. 'A civil funeral, they call it—they bury people like dogs in this country.'

It was Bea who said, 'But she was far too young to die from the heat!'

'Not the heat,' said the Queen of Hearts. 'The loneliness.'

Marie-Louise had even phoned Vlasta the night before

she did it and asked him to come into town. He told her to take a sleeping pill and go to bed. How the Queen of Hearts knew all this is anyone's guess. When Marie-Louise didn't turn up at work the next day, the Post Office called around and it emerged that she hadn't left her apartment.

I pictured the Queen of Hearts in full authoritative mode, a locksmith at her feet fumbling with instruments.

'She was lying on her right-hand side,' she hissed loudly, 'The stuff she took was on the bedside table.'

In a way, I thought, the Queen of Hearts' curiosity was healthier than any French attitude to family. Then, with considerable misgiving, I began to wonder if religion might not have a role to play after all. I was careful not to mention this to Bea.

Later, as we lay in bed studying the cracks in the ceiling that needed redecorating, Bea said, 'Just think of her going through that and us on a white beach in the Aran Islands.'

'I've decided Marie-Louise wasn't bonkers,' I said after a while. 'Everything is so complicated, it simply has to have a cause,' I told her.

She sat up on one elbow and looked me straight in the eye.

'Don't tell me you're going to fall back on Intelligent Design and all that? After complaining for all these years about how even Descartes leaned on God, in the end?'

I realized it was too late to wrench the subject away from the possibility of supreme beings. It dawned on me that Bea's was an anger built up over years of packing boxes and moving them with me and my career.

'*You* were the one who wanted to come to France—

because of ideas, because of the *Enlightenment*. You fled Ireland because of the priests! We moved here—lock, stock and barrel—because of *Reason*!'

By now Bea was yelling.

I tried to calm her by telling other stories by Marie Louise—her nightmare about being pursued into a room full of furnaces and another about lining up for punishment by burning. 'I was always with other people, always accompanied,' Marie-Louise had said.

Bea rolled her eyes. 'Please, Frank,' she said. 'Don't start.'

'We humans are hard-wired to want lies,' I plunged into ever deeper water. 'Lies plug the breaches we find in causality. When we don't have answers, we content ourselves with lies. Fictions and stories comfort us, where the truth—the absence of a cause, the lack of a reason—would disturb us.'

I warmed to my subject. Bea turned away from me and got out of bed.

'Cave paintings were stories people told themselves about themselves too,' I said, as she closed the bedroom door behind her.

I'm Talking Too Much, Aren't I?

'Darling! Of all the gin joints in all the world! Wonderful to see you. What're you doing here? So long since you left St Pierre!

I'm here with a crowd—up for the weekend to celebrate the birthday of a gay friend I met on a train ten years ago. We counted it last night. We've been great friends since, although he's beginning to be a bit of a bore because he's been sitting in front of a computer for ten years and that's just too long. He organized this weekend in gay Paree with thirty-five friends, block-booked a hotel and paid for us all, and another American organized the party last night, champagne flowing and caterers in and all. We're just working it off now. The whole thing is mad. I'd only just gone back to the Vaucluse, but I decided to come up for it anyway. They're all younger than me but I didn't feel like a mother hen at all.

You and yours all well?

My son Anton's success in New York still has me bowled over—the fruit of my loins is a novelist!—the novel got a four-star review in the papers, which is really good but me and Anton had a big fight and I said in revenge you can't go to the house in the Vaucluse but then we made it up, because I realized it was either that or see even less of him, and after all I'll be fifty soon—again!—and he lives in New York. So then I relented and he came to Ste Eulalie after all and filled the house with young Americans. Anton is wonderful, of course he still has all those phobias, but he has that cheeky smile and, hey, take a look at these photographs. One evening he stood up—just like that—and read parts of his new novel for the company and it was terrific. He told me he once found himself in a sauna with eight women and he said to the girl next to him, "I'm the only guy here," and she said, "I'm the only straight girl!"

I'm also ecstatic about having earned enough money this year to put a pool in at the house in St Eulalie (an architect friend will do the drawings free in exchange for free stays and Njiro will do the work although I haven't asked him yet). The whole money thing started through something I designed for an auction for charity in the 16th arrondissement and the opening happened on St Patrick's Day and I just went in and although the place hadn't been done up or anything they were all there, Irish from everywhere, the Ambassador and all, there was even one called Ben who said, "I should be called Patrick really because it's my birthday today." And they kept saying, "This is the designer," like I was really important when they introduced me around and I laughed and they were so nice and so enthusiastic, all these Irish people. One of them asked if I hadn't a drop of Irish blood and I said I might. Then because of the free work I'd done, Irish people who live in France with lots of dosh—yes, well plenty of them are still well off, you know—just booked me for loads of work, although of course I didn't do it for that. I asked one of them, "What do you do?" and he said "I import eels to sell to the French"!

I'm coping better with Leila's thought disorder. Now it's

not a brain disorder as such but a variant of schizophrenia, for example see the pepper and salt cellars there, well, if you had a thought disorder you'd say for example one is the man and the other is the woman, but then you'd carry on with the thing from there in a logical progression like asking, for example, Why is the man wearing a hat because the salt cellar has a black top. It just gets completely barmy. You know she wanted to kill me and sometimes the police ring and say she's gone missing again and I say how the fuck can this happen but then this is much better than when she was in a squat and turning up from time to time in the street bawling. Anyway, that summer of the great heat wave, she stopped taking her medication altogether and finished up in a right pickle, fire- and ambulance-men round to the house, the whole bit. Finished up in a clinic for months. I'm thinking of sending her to a place in Belgium where they're treated like humans, encouraged to paint and play music and spend lots of time outdoors, plenty of living space and freedom. Lock her up, but humanely, you could say.

I think a thought disorder is also what my recently deceased father had. I tried to help him bring some order to the chaos of his affairs; he decided I was in fact trying to rob him. So I've just given up really. Leila's now a diabetic as well, more or less abandoned by her Polish man, he spends all his time building and she spends all her time whining by email or stuck in self-help books. She sent me a list of reading for New Year and there was only one reference on there that wasn't a self-help thing—took an overdose of insulin last winter in an attempt to kill herself. Somebody found her lying in a pool of vomit. Didn't work because she'd drunk a

150

lot of liqueurs in order to prepare herself for the thing and that saved her since they're full of sugar. So I said to her, I'm taking you to St Eulalie for New Year because I know that's a bad time for depressives.

You enjoying Paris?

As soon as I leave Ste Eulalie I realize how wonderful a place it is, city pollution gives me a migraine. St Eulalie is the ideal place for re-sourcing yourself on walks like up to the Hermitage or just sitting looking at the river or the wonderful river gorges. I need these times. You might think I just like drinking and sitting round in cafes and generally being in a crowd, but I'm really a gregarious hermit. Jung— was it?—introversion and all that.

I love my roof terrace in Ste Eulalie too, also paid for by cash-in-hand design work. Only the other day I was out there having my breakfast coffee and saw a boar burst through the undergrowth and I said to myself, Just imagine that, a boar in my garden—and past his bedtime!

Jeannine? She's fine, her relationship with Paul is over— the work is a bit problematic but I'm helping by giving her tutorials. I don't call it that to her face, of course, but I make her talk about the work for up to three hours at a time. I make suggestions about showing not telling, that kind of thing, and doing more of the shorter novels because those big historic things are antediluvian. That last short book was masterful but I don't care for those longer ones at all.

Jean-Pierre and Marianne still invite you to dinner and then spoil the great food by drinking too much and fighting with each other throughout the evening. He is wonderful, very funny, although probably was a bit of a bastard in the

past, always off with the lads leaving Marianne at home
and now they're down there in that small village and he'll
go slowly out of his mind. He paints well but can't finish
anything because he's an alcoholic, of course. That last big
exhibition with the dark greens and greys was a reflection
of his life, you know. Their daughter is down there after yet
another breakdown, fat as a fool, eating to beat the band, a
path worn from fridge to table. They've bought her a house
in another village but she refuses to move out to it. She
thinks they should split up and live one in each house but
they think she's mad. Marianne is still the same American
pretending to be English—you know that accent she has.
She even found some connection between their family name
and some aristocratic family in England. Now isn't that just
typical? But when you get her on her own she's great. We
took the TGV up here the other day—that merciless hot
day they had the strike. I had a big container of wine for the
party and it was so crowded there were people sitting in the
luggage racks. You know those seats for four people in the
middle of the carriage? Well I put Marianne sitting there and
just said, 'Don't you move even if they bring in an elderly
person on a stretcher.' Marianne just gulped and did what she
was told. I said I'd kill for a glass of wine and Marianne said
'Oh, but you can't,' and I said, 'Wait here.' So I went off and
got one of those, you know, the French plastic water bottles
and cut the top off it and turned part of it out to make a
spout and got out, you know, my big container of fifty liters
of wine and filled it. Of course the wine splashed all over the
place onto the floor and everything but I didn't care although
Marianne was worried she was also glad of the wine and in

fact got quite tiddly. I was melting, so I just slipped out of my underwear there and then on the train—let down the shoulder straps and just shucked the whole lot out at my feet the way we used to do in boarding school. Marianne said, 'Well you've certainly got the attention of the whole carriage now and no mistake.'

What else? That guy with the ponytail died of a heart attack. Olivier has a lover of fifty-seven. Catherine is still the same wanker, now quite mad, tits down to her knees. Made a piece of furniture for me after my own design, took three years to make and would have been suitable for the Hotel de Ville, especially if they had shares in some poison against woodworm, as I told her. Hubby still in computers, makes frequent trips to Silicon Valley then off in the other direction to India, where he trains the people who're going to take all our jobs without even leaving home to do so.

See that Misha over there, the one with the high cheekbones? Such a sweet, dreadful accent though. David's boyfriend, from Siberia. You know nobody ever lived in Siberia until Stalin shunted them all up there. Well his father came over to Ste Eulalie last year and during a party at my house he went up on the roof terrace and bawled at the sky. It was deafening and powerful, and you know Misha is now grieving because he went back to Siberia and committed suicide. Couldn't take all that change in the USSR and everything breaking up. You know the other night Misha said to me, 'No woman can do a Cossack dance because they can never get their legs high enough or apart enough,' and I said, 'Yes they can' because I never let anyone away with saying I can't do anything and so I did the splits and Misha was amazed and I was delighted but

I really did hurt myself. The Irish contingent is quite strong here - I found myself walking along the street the other night with them and one of them just burst into song and I said to myself, "This is amazing—these people are total strangers..."

I'm talking far too much aren't I?

Ah, here's Marianne now—I get the impression we're off. Darling, we had no time to talk about you...'

MASTERY

The mixture that is not shaken soon stagnates
- Heraclitus

Monsieur Pierre is a vendor in a furniture store, not far from Place de la République in Paris's teeming north-eastern quarter. In the evenings, when the other vendors have left, the owner confides the store to him before heading off for an apéritif. This is the moment when Monsieur Pierre removes his black jacket and sits on the high stool at the counter, resplendent in his white shirt. People going home on wet streets are struck by his solitude, absorption and control. He reads up on new products and materials, sometimes looking up from his work to survey the furniture and the shop, as if it were all part of his own home.

No one knows much about him and only his employer actually knows if Pierre is his first name or his family name. Something about him suggests another time and place: His head and pale skin retain a boyishness; his high cheekbones have the slight blush of one who lives outdoors. His hair too is that of a boy, with what the barber calls an ear of corn at the front—a quiff which sticks up in spite of the creams and lotions he uses to control it.

Invariably dressed in a black suit and snow-white shirt, his manner suggests something of a lackey. This is reinforced by a tendency to wring his hands, particularly when elucidating

155

the finer points of the products he sells, or when he senses a sale is close.

Monsieur Pierre's look belies the fact that he is an expert in the hard sell. He has mastered all the skills and products and can read customers like a book. They are reassured by his penetrating eyes and boyish looks, incapable of suspecting anything but honesty and sincerity. He plays this to the utmost, often calling the store manager to vouch for some of the facts or prolong a special offer, and give the customer time to think. The manager respects these ploys and plays the game. Monsieur Pierre holds the store record for sales and commission. The other vendors say he could sell sand to Arabs, yet few of them actually see him in any other light than the customers: that of a boyish, put-upon hard worker.

Only after closing time does Monsieur Pierre take on a different air, master of all he surveys among the elegant sofas and occasional tables. He prefers certain styles, particularly likes old-fashioned English furniture—he is expert at suggesting to customers where a piece might best fit and what fabrics might match. He gleans information and ideas from a stock of magazines and catalogues he keeps under the counter and sometimes whips out to clinch a sale.

Recently he has noted, but oddly doesn't mourn, the fact that most of the elegant stuff is disappearing. Things are rapidly changing in the neighborhood. Most elderly people of modest but tasteful means have died or gone into homes. Smaller apartments in rundown buildings are being taken over by a young new breed, who want just a minimum of practical furniture that folds away against the walls, with maybe a transparent telephone or a neon clock. These are trendy twenty-to-forty year-olds who consider themselves 'zen,' who move house with a friend's van, leave stuff they no longer want under a tree for the city to remove, then buy their new needs afresh and cheaply, choosing style before comfort. They rarely spend much time at home anyway, and prefer to hang out with friends in *tapas* bars and cheap restaurants up and down rue Oberkampf.

Monsieur Pierre himself lives on the top floor of one of these old buildings, in a tiny room painted entirely in white (except for a brown patch on the ceiling due to a leaking roof). He keeps his room impeccably tidy. Its sparse furniture bears no relation to the kind he likes to sell, except for a valuable carved desk in dark wood that he found at a street market and which he suspects might have been stolen. Sometimes in the evenings he just sits and admires it, which is what he is doing this evening when his concierge, Fernande, knocks on the door. She has news, other than the state of the building and the impossibility of its inhabitants paying for restoration.

'Two guys,' she says, breathlessly. 'Location scouts, they called themselves. For a film.'

Monsieur Pierre indicates the kettle and raises an eyebrow. Fernande nods. Mr Pierre puts water on for tea. He likes having someone to share tea with, although he knows Fernande prefers coffee. It means he can take out his best pot and tea set.

'It'll help me sleep. I fueled up on coffee all day,' she says. 'Listen, they could save the building, these people. The film is to star Matt Damon, they said.'

Mr Pierre recognizes the name from bus-stop posters as he walks to and from work.

'Some kind of a thriller, with car chases.'

Mr Pierre still can't understand how the film will save the building.

'Try and keep up,' Fernande says impatiently. 'They want to use the yard and the porch entrances for a car chase. Shooting, they call it. A Mini Cooper or something like that—a Swatch wouldn't go quick enough. We're on their shortlist. They were very enthusiastic. One was French, he was the translator.'

Monsieur Pierre thought a Swatch was a Swiss watch. He imagines chaos in the yard beneath his windows, overturned dustbins, petrol fumes. He has already seen what filming can do to streets in the quarter, blocking cars and pedestrians. Busy types in black bearing walkie-talkies have frequently forced him to take another route to work. He thinks this shouldn't be allowed, and says so.

'But that's the whole point,' says Fernande. 'They pay for the service! We kept at them till they gave me a figure. It'd be enough to re-do the roof—imagine!'

She goes into detail about the roof and the scouts and Matt Damon until the teapot is empty. Monsieur Pierre ushers her out, reminding her that he will be away for the long weekend.

'I'll keep your mail, so,' she shouts as she goes down the stairs. 'Have a great time! Maybe I'll have more news by the time you get back!'

Monsieur Pierre sighs and closes his door, thinking that the whole building is now aware of his movements, something he dislikes intensely. It occurs to him that his years of peace and habitual routine are coming to an end, and that he may have to make a move soon.

From his everyday preoccupations Monsieur Pierre takes regular and spectacular breaks. He never discusses details of where he goes and colleagues have long since learnt not to ask. Every chance he gets, Monsieur Pierre goes on hunting trips to Morocco with a small group of acquaintances. Sometimes they go for a long weekend. Most of their trips focus on fishing, boar-hunting and falconry. This coming weekend, with a holiday and a *pont*—a bridge to a public holiday—is to be a grand festival of all three.

The group includes three brothers, two cousins, and Monsieur Pierre. The only thing he has in common with them is that they all live in Belleville, a quarter teeming with immigrants, many from North Africa. They met by accident on an early trip and have hunted together ever since. Monsieur Pierre is nonetheless aware of a difference between him and them: they are *pieds noirs*, cultural colonials of European origin, born in Morocco and dragged away from it by parents frightened by the Algerian war and Moroccan independence. For them each trip to North Africa is returning to paradise. Without these trips they would stop breathing. They have recently begun bringing their sons, so that they too will keep up the tradition: home is *là-bas*. 'down there.' France is some kind of temporary abode. That, and their mastery of Moroccan dialect, makes them closer to the locals, more familiar with the music and customs, all of which serves to keep Monsieur Pierre apart—which, up to now, is where he has preferred to be.

On Thursday the friends fly out early with Royal Air

Maroc, land near the desert, have a tasty lunch and take off for a lazy afternoon accompanying a snake-hunter on his rounds. Fascinated by his skill, they watched him tire, fool, and mesmerize serpents under the hot sun. Each time the snake-hunter reaches the crucial moment and slides shut the lid of his long wooden box, the friends watch carefully. Even when he releases the snake and starts again, to show them, they never quite manage to catch the detail of how he finally whips the snake into the box.

Monsieur Pierre finds himself becoming irritated and cannot work out why. A part of his mind, the non-hunter part, wonders again and again why the snake doesn't just cut and run at one of those moments while it is still free.

'How does he do it?' the friends marvel.

'Can't tell—he moves too fast,' another says.

'The snake helps out, he takes cover in the box,' Mr Pierre says quietly.

The snake-hunter nods. The snake takes rapid refuge in the very place that will become its prison until it is sold on to a snake charmer and turns up on Jemaa-el-Fna, the main square in Marrakesh, dancing to flute music, mastered for life.

Next day they fish for hours from the rocks at the edge of the broad Atlantic, cool even on a hot day in gumboots and capes against the salt spray, braving the elements with every wave that hits. Around them, Moroccans go to sea and lose their lives for fish. Behind them, other Moroccans help carry boats up to the safety of caves they have carved out of the higher cliffs. Beautiful women, enveloped in pale pastel colors, each with a child on her back, collect mussels they will boil and sell in the market in blue and white striped bowls, with a big safety pin for picking out the flesh.

Everyone but the foreigners avoids the dangerous area where the rocks meet the water, for these rocks are really the top of high cliffs concealed beneath treacherous waters.

'One slip means death!' the friends warn each other. They know how to be careful, and although always vulnerable to what nature can do to them, they know Nature is master.

Later they barbecue and share with locals the dozens of sea-bream they have caught. The others eat, laugh, and talk while Monsieur Pierre, as usual, finds himself hunkered before the barbecue, silent. He does most of the cooking, and eats last.

Next day they go boar-hunting. Monsieur Pierre's companions treat the locals as a race apart, refer to them as 'they,' give them instructions in Arabic and speak about them, in their presence, in French.

'They're in their Sunday best,' one says.

Although they are poor, it is clear that the local men have dressed up for the occasion: Monsieur Pierre's companions have stipulated that everyone must wear natural, non-vivid colors. Monsieur Pierre studies the poor men who arrive in oddments of sport and casual wear that probably took quite an effort to obtain.

The beaters, guided by one of the locals from the top of a dead tree, spread out against the hill, driving the forbidden meat towards the infidel hunters. The man in the tree yells instructions. The beaters yelp replies to each other and to the friends waiting with the guns.

Monsieur Pierre feels as if he has moved through a glass

wall to find himself mysteriously on the side of the victim, but to no obvious purpose and with no sale in view.

That evening they have car problems. By nightfall they find themselves and their four-wheel drive in the filthy garage of a very elderly Portuguese in a small town on the edge of the desert.

'Great to have someone to talk to,' the old man says, through stumps of teeth and gums. 'Been here all my life. Quarter used to be full of Europeans like me. Small businesses.'

Monsieur Pierre's companions are silent, perhaps conscious that here—but for their parents' decision in the 1960s—had lain their own fate.

The old man barks harsh commands in Arabic to his latest assistant, a young man from the new apartment blocks, who struggles with the unfamiliar vehicle, sweating heavily under their combined gaze.

'Big trouble holding onto them,' the old man shakes his head. 'Look at the way he works. They just don't have the reflexes.'

The others nod. Monsieur Pierre doesn't react.

It is late when the repairs are complete.

'Sorry,' the old Portuguese man says, asking for what, in Euros, is small change: 'prices on the rise.'

As they turn the car and drive away, Monsieur Pierre watches the old man close his black garage and make his stiff way back to a house which is small and poor just like all the others in a street and quarter that is now full of Moroccans and not foreigners.

☙

Back in Paris, Fernande springs on Monsieur Pierre as he enters the hall.

'The film people want us to supply water and electricity,' she announces officiously. 'Won't that be easy, out here in the yard? The building council is having a meeting to count up the cost and the gains. They have a lawyer examining the contract. Big fancy thing with an address in California.'

It seems she has set the whole quarter alight with film jargon. The word on the street is that Matt Damon will save the decrepit roof. The excitement and the news stir only a feeling of insecurity in Monsieur Pierre. The brown patch on his ceiling seems to be growing.

During the following week, fellow-workers are surprised to notice Monsieur Pierre make fewer sales. A stunning white sofa that was ordered through him with a down payment hasn't been collected or paid for by the deadline. He has to go through the ignominy of phoning the would-be purchasers and being told they've changed their mind—they don't want it. Even the paperwork involved in keeping their deposit grates on his nerves.

When he arrives in from work on Saturday evening he is tired. He feels that he needs time to think. He wonders if all places, in time, turn out to be traps.

Fernande comes rushing up the stairs, almost in tears.

'They voted against us! The council was too greedy! They chose another quarter for the film—oh, it'll be made in Paris all right. How are we ever going to save the roof now?'

Monsieur Pierre forces tea on her but doesn't drink much of it himself. When she is gone he finds himself wondering how much he would get for his desk if he were to sell it.

When Sunday comes around he joins his hunter friends in an old house with a garden at the top of Belleville, for what they laughingly call 'Lunch on the grass.'

When he has carefully prepared the barbecue, Monsieur Pierre wanders down steps into a hut in the garden and watches one of the hunters teach his son to make his own bullets.

'*Regarde, mon fils,*' the man says. Watch, my son.

There is a little measure for just the right weight of pellets, and a machine that compacts the powder then seals the capsule in the shape of a star.

Monsieur Pierre examines the objects thoughtfully. He feels a vicious stab of jealousy towards this man, with a distinct history behind him and a son to carry on after him.

Both father and son look at Monsieur Pierre. '*He's* a good hunter too,' the father tells his son.

For the first time, it strikes Monsieur Pierre that his friends never refer to him by name. He *is* a good hunter, but he isn't one of them. Images of the furniture shop and the snake in the box flash before him. Mastery is a layered cake, he thinks. And he wonders if it is too late now to shift levels.

He returns to set the barbecue alight. The women bring out salads and bread. A child takes a photo of them all and a digital camera is passed around. Monsieur Pierre sees, as in a hallucination, his own pale face staring out from the family tableau of tanned likenesses, smiling like an idiot child.

༄

Two years later the whole quarter flocks to see the new Matt Damon film. There are car chases and Parisian buildings, but nothing looks at all like their quarter, and none of the buildings are remotely run-down. Fernande says films like that are not her thing anyway, although she wonders if location scouts may not one day see her yard for the jewel that it is.

Lightning Strikes Twice

It is almost Halloween, behind the chalk cliffs of the Alabaster coast, much-loved of the Impressionists. On evenings like this I stand at my window and wait for my young researcher to turn up. I say 'my,' but of course Langlois visits others too. Indeed she seems to do little else all day long. She calls it work. She'll wheel up in a neat little brand-new car and park tidily in a corner of the yard, as if we were expecting a crowd.

If she still hasn't arrived when the light goes, I turn on the telly for company. At that time of evening there's just rubbish and games, but I like its eerie light. I put the volume up full too. There are no neighbors to complain, most of those roundabout have already died or left, although others are arriving. There are two Polish families. The castle farm's mostly automated now, with machines the width of the road and tractors like Airbuses that cost almost as much.

The family of our former Lord and Master has a goodly selection of these Airbuses, although all the comte ever really cared for was his horses. 'Bloodstock's the thing, Marie-Jeanne!' he used to say to me when I still worked up at the chateau. When he still spoke to me. Before they retired me from the castle farm to this little house. It's on the side of the road, but I don't complain because I like to see the odd passer-by. I counted two cars and three tractors today, and our new British residents, out for what they call their

166

'constitutional.'

The Poles, as factotums and farmhands, are better lodged than we ever were: the comte even restored two traditional stone houses for them, landscaped, the whole bit, overlooking a lake that provided power for the old forges. Original tiling, gutters, very pure and traditional altogether. No doubt he got subsidized to do so, for money always attracts money, as my brother liked to point out. The lake and forges kept the comte's ancestry rich and the rest of us in work. In the old days it was the only respectable job a noble could do apart from soldiering. The Poles'll not lack for fish this winter, although no one'll be any the wiser. They have three kids here, keeping our school from what was an inevitable shutdown, and several more at home doing military service and whatnot.

Bussed them in, did the comte, local unemployed notwithstanding ('Can't work, won't work,' he said). They are paid the minimum, and they're happy to do the work of ten. 'It's lots more than they'd get at home, and everyone's happy,' the comte said to me from his wheelchair the last day I spoke to him.

By the time Langlois comes, I'm deafened by the telly and tetanized by the evening light. So she knocks and yells and finally has to step into the firelight like a Christian and declare herself. I check on the cakes and biscuits she brings—we often have a sugar lump dipped in the home-made Calva I found all over the cellar after my brother was killed. Called a 'duck' locally, this amuses Langlois no end.

She's mad for all my news.

Langlois is researching coincidence. She heard about me

from her parents who used to raise pigs outside the village. They told her about the time I was struck by lightning. Then there was the foot falling down the comte's chimney into my pumpkin soup. That and a few more things and she had a path beaten to my door.

'Tell me about the lightning!' she cried that first day. 'Where were you when it hit you?'

That was easy to work back to, and anyway the ambulance men told me they found me in the middle of the field with the milk bucket in one hand and the milking stool still attached to my backside. I didn't believe them until the hospital staff concurred. *Concur* is a good word, often used by little blonde Langlois. She's very proper—her favorite coincidences concern St Thérèse of Lisieux, further south from here—so I have to make sure to avoid *patois* or crude words, else she looks consternated.

Fact is I was unconscious for three whole days. Severe burns down the entire side of my body. Fascinated that Rolande too was struck by lightning on her scooter, Langlois and I spent several evenings on the fact that me and Rolande feel alive with electricity when a storm is due, allowing us to predict the weather, but also making us nervous and irritable.

Later, when Langlois got wind of the burglar that died in the comte's chimney, I was guaranteed company for the whole winter. We've had researchers here before—it was about witchcraft the last time—and we know they like to spin it out. So I eked it out gently like the home-made Calva.

Where was I? These last days of a very late Indian summer are distracting with their warm southern winds. It's already shriveled up my Virginia creeper, red after an initial cold

168

patch. Anyway, the earth is parched after the summer. Wells are down to mud level, and this is the first time I've ever seen them harvest maize without strewing muck all over the roads.

So: the foot.

Langlois wasn't the first to visit me about the foot. When it first happened, I was still working at the chateau and the journalists, the telly, were all over the place—and me. A telly van with a special antenna parked down the road until the comte got his pals at the gendarmerie to shift them. 'Tell them what happened, Marie-Jeanne,' he said, 'no more, no less. Let us get them out of our hair once and for all, shall we?' You can see he'd be well able to chat to the Queen of England, who came over and stayed once. They had horseflesh in common. There's a photo of her still in the library, and a copy of the thank you letter she sent afterwards. (The new guide up at the chateau gets great mileage out of this, although you can tell tourists don't like her tight mouth, tight speech, tight clothes, and the big wallet she hugs tightly under her arm until she unlocks the last door to let them out, drawing their attention to a bilingual notice suggesting tips.)

So I told the story, again and again.

It was evening. I'd made the soup, tasted and seasoned it, added the cream. I'd put it under the big chimney in the corner, to the side of the big fire we'd only started lighting the day before. It was my only luxury, the fire, with its huge logs. The comte burns his own forests, of course. I had my own favorite armchair, and liked nothing better than to sip a bowl of hot chocolate there in the late afternoon, looking for faces in the flames.

I'd got used to the smell; we all had, over the previous days. It was unpleasant, but was thought to be a malfunction of the septic tank (in those days it was too near the house, the comte was waiting for European money—or money from anywhere—to move it, which he eventually did. There's now a spanking field of reeds that people come far and wide to see, as an example of How To Do It). The *pompe à merde* was whistled up like a shot by the comte. This spread another smell far and wide that masked the other one. 'Nothing wrong with that tank,' muttered Guérin when he'd done emptying it, 'there was a toad playing around the opening.' Guérin, with his conspiratorial air, is close to the earth. He also grows spuds and sells them from the back of his van. Indeed he looks a little like a spud man with a little red spud nose. 'I presume that fellow lacks any sense of smell,' the comte once said.

When that wider odor dissipated, the more sinister one just came back again. While all this was going on, I was up to my neck in work at the chateau, twenty-four hours non-stop with all their demands and hot water bottles against the chill because they were back from frolicking in warm water in foreign parts.

Then my brother killed himself in his car, late at night. Suddenly I was also milking his goats and feeding his hens as well.

No one knew—least of all me—where he was going when he crashed, so late at night, and with a packed valise in the car boot.

I only got suspicious when the police started sniffing around, asking too many questions. I didn't give them the benefit of my opinions—we might have sat on the same primary school benches, but they'd gone further. Let them work it out, if they were that smart.

I buried my brother. Even the priest was reluctant to show up, on the grounds that he was too busy, with seventeen parishes to cater for. So I changed the day, upped the money, and forced the priest to bury him. And may the devil punish all of his ilk.

My brother was no good, but I had to give him a good send-off.

The church was so packed that day there were people standing in the aisle. And when they filed up to bless the coffin and leave a coin, we even got a laugh. A tourist, mistaking the long holy water thing the undertaker proffered for something else (same shape—I always thought—as hospital pisspots for men), inserted his coin into it. The coin disappeared with a glug, and people around her tried to keep from exploding.

Back to the foot.

The soup was the comte's required *velouté*, the quail were within minutes, when there was a rustling in the chimney. It became a rush and suddenly something fell with a plop into my soup. It fell shoe first with the bone sticking up, so that at first I thought this the stable boys' idea of a joke.

Then I realized what it was and—well, I screamed.

Hours later the chateau was still full of gendarmes and people like spacemen in lab suits. They'd called the roofer and managed to extricate the rest of the body from the chimney, but it took them hours of yelling up and down and in and out. The quail dried up, my soup went to a lab in Caen, and while waiting for the police, the comte and his family ate packet soup surreptitiously in their separate kitchens, as they do when they're fighting (it happens). A cat got into the bedrooms with muddy paws, guaranteeing work for me and the Miele for weeks. 'And were you shocked, and frightened?' (thus Langlois). I didn't tell her I ate hazel nuts from the store I'd collected in the fields and ditches, once I got my appetite back.

It took weeks for the police to inform even the comte, who eventually informed me that the dead man was from an hour away in another county, a known burglar and part of a team that specialized in chateaux burglaries. He'd obviously got stuck in the chimney and taken days to die. The period in question corresponded with the time the comte and his family went abroad and I was free of the kitchen for a while.

What the police couldn't work out was the identity of his accomplice, becauseonce safely inside, he was obviously meant to open doors and let someone else in to help load the stuff.

It was here that I made Langlois work. I never drew her attention to the main coincidence, but she got to it eventually: my brother's accident coincided with the time the comte was abroad. When she finally did get to it, I defended him roundly and acted offended. There was no proof anywhere. But I knew my brother had to be rushing for help when he got killed. Otherwise he'd have told me, wouldn't he? Got me to help?

All I can think of now is the state of mind of the poor devil in the chimney: first thinking my brother was going to save him; then thinking he'd chickened out; finally believing he'd been betrayed.

My hair was white already, so it couldn't go white again.

Last week the count died, and it rained and rained. The comtesse stuck notices to the door of every church in the county to say that he was lying in state in the chateau chapel and wouldn't be interred for a week. It poured rain the day of the actual interment, and when the Mass was over the comtesse handed out photos of our Lord and Master as a memento. Politicians and local figures were inside the small chapel and dry, us plebs stayed out in the damp on the lawn under a specially-erected tent that the comtesse referred to as a marquise, among official cars bearing little red-white-and-blue flags and lorry-loads of wreaths. It was all a far cry from my brother's funeral.

I've kept the comte's photo. I have time to reflect on memory, and on coincidence. I think of all those who once respected the Comte of Stone and those few remaining who still do. I think of the Poles: they must surely fit in well here, late as they are of a society based on discipline and obedience, and Catholic to boot. I see little of them, but when I do I notice their cheap tracksuits and meek, obsequious, eager-to-learn look, with something like cunning at the back of it. I look at the new arrivals to the village, young and rich or young and penniless, at the increasing numbers of Brits in their new playground. And I wonder how we will all cope with this new, comte-less autonomy, this new world where Me comes first...

I think Langlois' book is an effort to cope with at least

some of that.

They installed a pacemaker recently under my skin, a hard thing, big as a matchbox. They have told me not to use a mobile phone or, if I have to, not on that side. They have told me not to travel by plane. As I told them, I have no use for planes or mobiles. I often imagine the next storm may carry me off, and dread the advance sensations it will bring.

Last night I dreamed that my brother was here, so lifelike I could swear I got a whiff of his smelly hunting dogs. I asked and he told me about life on the other side. 'There's nothing,' he threw his hands wide, 'just nothing.' I made him say it again and again. Would it not depend on your belief? I wanted to ask timidly. But before I could do so, he vanished.

FRANK STANDS HIS GROUND, IN BELLEVILLE

Die Wüste wächst: weh Dem, der Wüsten birgt!
- Nietzsche: *Also Sprach Zarathustra*

Frank struggled from sleep. The lights were on. Bea was pulling at his shoulder.

He struggled to understand. It was still dark. It was August. It was holidays. They had been out late with friends. Had she gone mad?

'Get up, quick!' she hissed. 'There's a fire in the café!'

On the ground floor of their building, the café was a comfortably shabby place with a corner bar, over which two fat North African ladies presided. Neighbors often complained about the noise from the jukebox—mostly North African or '60s & '70s music—but Frank loved it, and the crowd that went with it.

He went through his inventory again. He could hear nothing, except the open-windowed summer night's calm, when everyone finally sleeps.

'Get up!' Bea ordered again, more urgently this time.

He was about to argue when he heard it, from the street below:

'Au feu! Au feu!' Then again: *'Le gaz, levez-vous!'*

As he struggled to drag on trousers against his own sleepy awkwardness, he said, 'But there's no smell, not like last time.'

'I've already been down,' Bea said. 'There's smoke coming from the kitchen.'

This was as good as a shot of caffeine to him. He scrambled into shorts and a tee-shirt.

Last time there had been a fire in the street they'd smelled it first and called the fire brigade. 'Are the flames coming out the window yet?' the fireman had asked calmly. Flames must be a criterion of some kind, he reassured himself as he headed down the stairs.

Since then the quarter was looking up: parking had been banished and footpaths widened. Some buildings had been done up. Trendy new cafes abounded. But the overall impression still was of a shabby islet in a tremendously rich city.

Down on the street people had begun to gather. There was discussion about how to contact the owner. Someone went off to get a mobile phone number.

Suddenly a fire engine nudged into the narrow street, and all hell broke loose.

One of the firemen approached Frank's door and stairs: 'You live here? Come with me,' he was told.

They met Bea on the way down. The fireman told her to go down and stay down.

They started at the top of the building. Windows were open on the stairs to catch any breath of summer wind. There was a whiff of urine from the communal toilets. The fireman questioned Frank about the number of inmates in each apartment before banging loudly on each door, checking numbers and ordering the occupants downstairs on the double. He didn't bother to ring or knock, just hammered with all his might. Nor did he allow any questions, just repeated firmly to surprised and sometimes angry occupants— reassured by Frank's presence—to get out, there was a fire in the building and that this was orders. Frank remembered that firemen were part of the army, and felt a chill.

On the second floor, there was no reply from one of the doors. The place was supposed to be for sale, friends of Frank and Bea wanted to buy, but the owner refused even to let them visit. Frank reckoned this was a cover for something.

Next to it, the Tunisians nodded obediently and prepared to exit the building. Whenever he heard the rattle of their backgammon, Frank was always reminded of a Raymond Chandler private eye and the seedy hotels he frequented, where music and fights leaked out over transoms. But Chandler had never seen anything quite so rundown as this.

Frank wavered between amusement and utter despair at the broken panes that opened onto a stinking light-well. Everything stank. Residents making their way up the stairs came eye-level, twice, with the toilets whose cleaning depended on their users. Both remained ajar, and disgusting. Only yesterday as he made his way down, a small cat crept out from an abandoned mattress and skipped through the Tunisians' door. 'What the hell is that?' a voice from within asked, in Arabic. 'A bloody cat!' said another. 'Salop'rie!' both voices cried together. Frank knocked and stood back discreetly, the way they do in North Africa. The Tunisians invited him in, to explain recent building management bills. Two sets of bunk beds sat on either side of some ten square meters. In one corner a sink was surrounded by washed crockery. To one side of it, on a one-fire gas burner, simmered a pot emitting sensational aromas. The two men wore stained *djellabahs*. The third, the son of one of them, lay on a top bunk where he was recovering from a leg injury received on a building site where he had been working illegally, as a change from not working at all down in Tunisia.

Frank often wondered where they washed themselves, let alone their clothes, and felt a pang of sorrow for their lives, their wives, their children, and even for their short and boring retirement which would be mostly spent on a bench up the street in Belleville. One of them already spent Saturdays sitting on a stone outside the yard door.

They drank tea and eventually Frank brought up the subject of their families *'là-bas.'* Down home. They dutifully showed him the photos, the richly-decorated salons, the new village water-pump and mosque paid for with emigrant contributions. Frank asked if they missed it all. They fell about laughing. 'No way! We have enough trouble dealing with them by phone! They only contact us to ask for money. Oh no—we're nice and quiet here.'

Frank had remounted the stairs thoughtfully that day, thinking that the world was full of surprises.

When he and the fireman had roused all the occupants, the fireman ordered Frank outside as well.

'But I need to close up, collect a few essentials,' he stuttered. Passport, money, access to money ran through his head.

The fireman blocked his way, hands out. 'Downstairs with the others. Now. This is not a game, *monsieur.'*

Frank was furious. He had thought he was helping, now

178

he realized he was being used.

Bea was standing with a crowd of scantily clad neighbors from their own and other buildings, watching the firemen rush about. There was still only a rope of smoke in the café itself, emanating from the minuscule kitchen in the back. No one had yet been able to contact the owners or get a key. It started to drizzle. Frank remembered the black and white photos of post-war stars of stage and screen adorning the café that had been bought years back from a gruff provincial who also sold coal and sticks. It had changed hands and habits overnight without as much as a lick of paint.

There was a ripple at the edge of the quiet crowd as the older of the two Algerian women in bright clothes finally turned up. A loud altercation ensued between her and the firemen, with help from onlookers, in Arabic—or was it Berber? —and French. She had been sleeping in a neighboring building. It turned out she was not the owner, merely the minder of the café/bar, and didn't have the key. The owner, it emerged, was the rough-looking Serb who served early coffees in the mornings. Frank had taken him for just another taciturn waiter. Now it turned out he also came late at night to take the cash and close up for the night. Frank marveled at how little he really knew of the workings of the quarter.

With maddening slowness, the firemen began to hack at the door of the café with what looked like large hatchets. The noise woke more and more people in other buildings, bringing them down onto the street. Gradually the café filled with black smoke.

Bea was building herself into a state of nervous tension. 'The windows,' she wailed, 'all the windows are open! I don't even have a pullover!'

'Why the hell don't they go through the broken window to the side?' someone said. A sheet of glass was cracked from a bar fight a month or two earlier.

'This is France,' said another, 'rules probably say you have to go through the door.'

'My lovely apartment!' cried Bea.

Frank shivered. They'd only just finished painting it. Bea hadn't always thought it lovely when they'd moved from a bigger, flashier one. But this way he could continue painting and they could pay the bills. Bea could play around in her workshop, creating designer garments for the young, trendy and not-so-rich of the 10th arrondissement.

He began to think of the consequences if they didn't control the fire. What if the whole building went up? Stranger things had happened. They might have been lucky to get away with their lives. Sometimes the occupants of an entire Paris building inhaled smoke and died in their beds. Occasionally gas exploded and a whole tenement collapsed. Everything they had was up there. He thought of the trouble there would be to replace paperwork and residence permits.

The rain got heavier. Friends from other buildings went for umbrellas and jackets. One sheltered Bea and gave her his last Lucky Strike. *Greater love than this*, Frank thought, and vowed to keep an eye on that one in the future.

'Always wondered what you do when I'm gone home for the night!' a voice said laughingly in his ear.

It was Djilali, a café regular, who lived at the top of the

street. Frank always reckoned Djilali never slept anyway. Of indeterminate age, oriental origins, possessing the smoothness and money of a rich man, his life was a mystery to Frank. He had a young (second) wife, whom he watched like a hawk, berating young men on the street if they 'lacked respect' for her, as he put it. He also had a beautiful daughter reaching puberty for whom he had purchased a mobile phone, 'To keep track of her. World ain't what it used to be.' Frank thought Djilali would know plenty about the world.

The two men shook hands. They had always maintained a steady but distant friendship, but only in the café, as Bea didn't like him.

Djilali observed the firemen at work. 'Anti-vandal glass,' he said. 'That'll take a while.'

Frank thought it odd that a lousy café such as this should go to the trouble of installing special reinforced glass doors. While he sometimes wondered if Djilali was into something really odd, he still reckoned he could count on him if he ever were in trouble. Frank did know where Djilali came from, because Djilali had once said, after an absence, 'Went to Ghardaia by plane from Oran, but they wouldn't allow me visit—sent me back to the hotel with the bus driver. And I'm Algerian, like them! They let the tourists in, and even two French grandfathers. But not me. They're that close down there.'

The fire engine ladder was extended, and hoses prepared to get water from the canal. A second and third fire engine nosed up the street.

Someone had remembered the Chinese, and the firemen began to hammer at the big steel door. No light could be seen over the heavily barred transom. Everyone knew about the ground-floor room, but Frank also knew that underneath it was a vaulted basement, for he once had to accompany the manager on a check of some kind. It was filled with rows of sewing machines.

This would be sport, Frank thought, for the Chinese never opened to anyone except another Chinese. You never saw them come or go, just the occasional suit with a briefcase, knocking and getting no reply. Even the roach-and-rat-killer didn't get in. 'Much use the rest of us paying for extermination,' Bea had grumbled, 'if there's a center of production in the basement.' This was an unusually mean comment, for Bea. It was a complex subject: the owner of the basement was one of the building co-owners, so they often found themselves at meetings with him, an equal of sorts. This irked Bea, who put him on the level of the other 'sleep merchants' of Belleville who rented crowded dormitories full of bunk beds. This one rented it through a Chinese agency, while renting all his other rat holes personally, getting what he called a 'big Malabar' from across the city limits in Aubervilliers to collect the rent. Frank had seen the 'Malabar': he was big and black and brooked no discussion. 'They pay the rent or they get out,' the owner told him.

It took nearly an hour for the firemen to break in the café door. When it finally flew open, black smoke billowed upwards and into all the open windows.

It could be a scene from Balzac, Frank thought, before Napoleon III instructed the Baron Haussmann to sanitize the city, demolishing left, right, and center and producing the Paris that everyone knew today.

Frank's architect friend Crollo (from his proper name, C. Rollo) had found their apartment for them, and had first told Frank about Haussmann. He pronounced it 'Ozman,' like they all did, so that at first Frank thought he was talking about a Turk. Paris had been medieval until Haussmann sorted it out. The odd thing was that their quarter had gone up precisely at the same time that Haussmann was knocking down tenements and putting up elegant apartments elsewhere. Crollo reckoned their buildings were built with material from a giant Haussmannian demolition tip. Even the beams in their apartment were second-hand. 'Just imagine what a quarter like this must have replaced,' Bea said. Here, in the center of town, some well-meaning soul had put up these modest but correct buildings for poor workers. 'So they could exploit them better,' said Crollo. The still-operational but much-ignored rules stipulated when clothes could be hung out and carpets beaten. Curiously, parrots had been forbidden to nineteenth-century workers.

Blue and orange flames suddenly broke out in the café, and firemen were silhouetted struggling before them, through the smoke. Frank imagined Humphrey Bogart and Michèle Morgan curling in the heat.

Bea and some of the women were getting into a terrible state. There was nothing Frank could do. He found he wanted to say nothing either. He knew he was a bad painter—it had taken him two years to finish a portrait of Bea. Oddly, he remembered his trunk of adolescent scribblings—it was up there, and it had traveled with him everywhere. It was crap, but he wanted to drool over it one more time. He wanted to clean out his cupboards and drawers and burn it all or take it all to the dump and then write one last thing that would last.

Djilali dug him in the ribs and signaled that he should listen to the conversation behind them.

'They do it for the insurance money,' a voice was saying. 'They can set the fire off at a distance.'

There were vague suggestions of how this could be done with modern technology. Frank recognized the speaker, an older man of some seventy years he often saw on the street. One day, pointing to a pool of urine on a footpath, the same man said viciously to Frank, '*Macaques*.' Frank was so surprised he said, 'What?' 'They're like monkeys,' the older man said, 'straight out of the jungle.' Frank had simply stared at him and walked on. He told himself he hadn't argued because there was no point, no possibility of being heard. Afterwards he realized it was a failure of nerve. Seeing the man again in the same mode, he was sufficiently annoyed to want to atone.

He turned to speak.

But Djilali caught his arm. He smiled and shook his head. He seemed to be amused.

'Half of them are illegal, too,' the old man went on.

The last item was true. In the café Frank often ran into young men who had slipped into the country and worked extremely hard to send money home, but who—without rental contracts and service bills—couldn't prove residence or apply for papers. They could go neither forwards or backwards, couldn't marry, couldn't relax vigilance, couldn't ever do anything like a normal resident. The café was the only place they could let go for a couple of hours. This was Frank's idea of hell. He presumed they weren't afraid to talk to him because he was a regular and on handshaking terms with the Algerian women and Djilali.

He caught Djilali's twinkling eye, and they both began to laugh.

An axe was being applied to the Chinese steel door. A light went on inside, and voices were heard crying out. The firemen made no language concessions, merely repeating what they'd said to Frank earlier, in French, finishing with the polite but menacing *'Monsieur'* or *'Madame.'*

The crowd stood back as firemen inside the cafe broke the reinforced plate glass windows and threw them into the street.

Bea began to cry, and was taken away by a neighbor for a change of clothes and hot tea. Frank nodded assent, but felt he couldn't get involved, that he had to stay where he was.

Suddenly he understood the graffito that was scrawled inside their hall door and attributed to Nietzsche: *The desert grows; woe to him who conceals deserts within himself.* At least he thought that was what it meant. His German was rusty. He had always thought the quote was destined wryly at the general situation of the building, the street, the quarter. He still saw it all rather like he had from the start: Dante's Inferno with the worst levels at the bottom of the hill, those tenements onto which the whole hill seemed to lean and drain, squeezing them into an agony of bulges and fissures, expansion and contraction, of buckling and dirt livened by the whispers of the army of parasites that lived off them all.

A long and winding street at the bottom, near the canal, was reputed to have once been part of Haussmann's *cloaca maxima*, a brand new drainage system modeled on the original one in ancient Rome. Frank could just see it, paved and concave in the middle for the sludge. Crollo also said that termites had heard the news and were on their way. He had seen them in other quarters: 'They go straight through concrete to get to a wooden beam on the other side.' Bea was terrified they'd have to pay a fortune *and* pump chemicals into the walls as well.

Architects could be frightening, Frank supposed, but he found Crollo strangely comforting. He lived around the corner in a similar apartment to theirs, his clothes dried on a wooden contraption hoisted over the bath. Crollo wasn't a bad architect, he was a practical one, and like some of the doctors and dentists on their side of town, he didn't go for fancy offices and fancy jobs. 'Everyone needs an architect like everyone needs a dentist,' he said. 'It's not the style of the waiting room that counts.' Crollo was a rare animal, a professional living in a real-time world of *Paris populaire*, shoveling shit and surprised at nothing.

Ten years ago as a fresh young architect Crollo had had trouble finding builders to work with him in the quarter. 'This can't be Paris!' the first one had declared. 'Whole thing should be bulldozed. Cracks and fissures I could stick my head in!' A builder Frank had called recently for an estimate persisted in thinking they were all tenants. 'City Hall own it?' the man enquired confidently. When Frank said they were owners, he laughed dramatically.

There had been a more sinister incident, when Bea went to the police to report the theft of her bike. 'You live *where*?' the policewoman asked, when she heard the address. 'You own or rent?' She looked genuinely shocked when Bea said they had bought. 'Sell, madame! Get out before it's too late!' Bea had come back clearly shaken. Frank suspected the police of wanting the status quo to remain—Them versus Us, without confusion from incoming Bobo-Lilies, as the newer bohemian-liberal occupants were dubbed.

He and Bea continued to cling to the side of the hill like everyone else. The population was now three times the density of the richer west side of town. In mid-nineteenth century, when these houses were built, it had only been double. But Crollo was optimistic in the early days, and continued to be so now. He presided over an association that prevented the whole thing from being demolished, disappointing developers ready to make a killing. One had threatened to take him up a dark alley. Crollo just laughed: 'People are tired of the '60s ghettos covered in white WC tiling. Militants are abroad. They have to move more cautiously. When he was Mayor of Paris, Chirac spent six hundred Euros a day on food. The mayor of another district got dead people out to vote.'

'If I were you, I'd watch my back on a dark night all the same,' Frank told him.

But Crollo was right, change was on the way. More and more young trendies were buying in. Young second-generation Arabs in the street spread rumors that these Bobo-Lilies used crack and cocaine and worked in TV. 'This place'll be as fashionable as the Marais soon,' they said, taking another drag on a joint. 'Who do you think we sell our dope to?'

Djilali's mobile rang. 'Gigondas or Chirouble?' he

pretended to reflect. 'Bring both,' he grinned.

'Ex-wife,' he explained. 'Has her own restaurant, just got rid of last customer. I've dinner ready for her. Likes to eat out in the early hours occasionally. Way to your ex-wife is through her stomach.'

Decidedly, Frank thought, Belleville was a very complicated place. He wondered if Djilali lived off his ex-wife.

Suddenly the large Chinese double steel doors were flung open. The scene inside resembled a theatre set. Top lit, the walls were lined with single beds with colorful bedclothes. On these, up to a dozen Chinese sat or lay in various positions, drugged from smoke and trying to wake up. The firemen didn't waste any time and soon these pale actors were helped off the stage, past the crowd. Without as much as a word or glance they headed off barefoot as for a definite destination. Frank hoped no one was sleeping in the cellar workshop.

'Beats the smell of durian, I suppose,' said a new voice. Crollo had arrived, at last, in a warm hooded jacket. He handed another to Frank.

'Enjoy the show,' said Frank bravely. He thought he might cry.

'They'll get it under control,' said Crollo. 'There's a lot worse than this.' He handed Frank a quart bottle of whiskey. They both took a swig then gave one to Djilali, who then headed off to meet his ex.

Bea had already had a run-in with the local youths. It had destabilized her. They had taken on many of the newcomers, especially those their own age. Especially the women. On hearing voices raised in the street Bea had shot down the stairs, arriving to find three young men harassing a middle-aged female blow-in about Bush and the war in Iraq. They had blocked her path and were showing her a photo from a website. 'What do you think of that, madame?' they were asking threateningly. Bea rode in to the rescue; there were words, and a good-looking young Arab in a white tracksuit came out of the café and threw a cup of coffee in Bea's face. She didn't back down, but continued giving them a piece of her mind, knowing that all this was a question of power and bluff and who could put on the most pressure. The young man continued shouting, but suddenly seemed to have invested all his ire in the coffee. Eventually it was he who backed down, especially when Djilali and others arrived.

After that Bea stopped taking part in local activities. She no longer supported Crollo's association. She became negative about what they might or might not do to improve anything. She wanted to create in peace, she said. This was no area to keep a boutique or open a restaurant, she said, although many were doing it. Whenever footsteps were heard running in the street, her ears pricked up and she waited to hear the inevitable cry of 'Stop, thief!' from a restaurant or an unsuspecting tourist.

Around four a.m. many people had decided to call it a day or found a place to sleep for a few hours. Frank and Crollo had finished the whiskey.

Suddenly there was a ripple among the spectators as they moved back to make way. Frank strained to observe a silent line of djellabah-clad men emerging in single file from the main door of the building. Eyes down, they quickly made their way through the crowd and melted into the night.

Crollo raised an eyebrow. 'Second floor,' Frank said. 'Has to be. It's the only apartment we didn't open up. Someone's raking rent in on the black.'

It was six a.m. before the firemen finished. Once they'd extinguished the fire, they tore out anything capable of smoldering on. Floors, ceilings, furniture sat in a glistening pile under the rain as the few people with work in the quarter made their way past.

Within days, the radio was reporting other fires in the poorer quarters of one of the richest cities in the world, fires in which people died and children suffocated in smoke before they ever had a chance to wake up.

Some insurance people came and interviewed everyone in the building about what they might have seen, who frequented whom, and who lived where. No one had anything much to say, although Bea made it her job to tell them anything she knew before the van came to move her stuff.

That autumn, trouble broke out all over the Paris suburbs. The media reported burnt cars in Clichy-sous-Bois and Montfermeil. Fires and destruction spread all over France and into Belgium and Germany. Each morning the media gave the growing numbers of cars burnt. Everywhere young men, like animals with stricken limbs, seemed to want to destroy part of themselves: their neighbors' cars, their own crèches, gymnasiums, schools, local associations. In Greece, young men set fire to car showrooms. By then Bea was good and gone, her brightly-fronted workshop all boarded up.

Yet the young men in Frank's quarter didn't react. Cars

burned as close as the 3rd and 17th arrondissement, but there was still no movement from their own hooded youths. Frank wondered if they'd perhaps smoked too much of their own product. He had no one to talk to at home, now that Bea had taken her homely and home-making affairs and what turned out to be most of the furniture. He found himself taking over her role in Crollo's association, attending interminable meetings with sociologists and politicians, and taking a certain pleasure in organizing a local festival.

He wondered if Bea would have to keep moving from arrondissement to arrondissement and from suburb to suburb to escape the hooded youths. Perhaps she would eventually stop and go home. Or perhaps she would encounter an elderly rich man who would supply her with all her worldly needs and a heavily-secured apartment on the Place des Vosges.

Frank decided to stay. He still wasn't sure if this was simply due to laziness and an inability to act, or the realization that this was his future, the motley crew that included himself, Djilali, Crollo, the two Algerian ladies, the Tunisians and the French, but also all the now-French kids of North African descent and their tired parents. It seemed to him the only way to deal with this was to stand. And talk.

For someone who had always favored silence, this was new.

᭪

It is summer's end. As evening changes to night this Saturday, Frank sits at his window and observes the street. The latest young man back from prison swings down the street in a white tracksuit to hang out with his friends. They greet each other North-African fashion, hand on heart. The ex-prisoner is missing several front teeth. Frank has seen young men like him before, more alive on their return than when they left, expert in the ways of the police, and very bitter.

The young men stand and watch half a dozen adolescents finish burning out a state-of-the-art scooter they have stolen, revving it noisily and scorching smokily up and down the street. Frank realizes that the young man in the white tracksuit is the one who threw coffee in Bea's face.

An elderly man with a beard hobbles by from a Saturday afternoon demonstration that finished locally. Many of the left-wing demos tend to finish on the north-east side of town, to avoid upsetting the bourgeois in the west. The man is carrying, upside-down, a poster that reads 'I hunger, therefore I exist!'

A girl tiptoes over a drainage grid in those extra-long pointy-toed shoes with needle-thin heels. Her trousers are over-wide. Her hair is dyed red. She is probably headed for a place where she can meet friends, many from the suburbs. At Bastille or Chatelet they will eat a deep-fried string that passes for calamari, served by young people like themselves. It will cost a fortune but they will consider it a good evening.

Frank thinks that is the best—perhaps the only—approach.

A Day on Rue du Faubourg

Morning

A Berber from Kabylia lays out chairs on the terrace of La Mandoline. The black man arranges papers and magazines at the front of his kiosk, climbs in through the back door, and waits. At the Hôpital St Antoine, Monsieur Tunc awaits Madame Nunquam, doing crosswords, never looking up. A North African, strongly resembling Kadafi, piles vegetables and fruit neatly on the stand before his small shop. The bar next door reads 'Closed.'

Afternoon

High in the hospital Monsieur Tunc does crosswords, never looking up. His wife embroiders quickly. No one speaks. Monsieur Tunc's drip drips regularly and, like him, is silent. The gipsy in the next bed sleeps, surrounded by his family, his children large-eyed and impressed. Their mother tells them God is good. Kadafi's lookalike dozes at the entrance to his shop. The small bar remains closed.

Dusk

On the hospital's fifth floor the gypsy's wife dozes in a chair beside his bed. Soon his colleagues will arrive to discuss business and she will leave. This big brown man leans on one elbow and stares into the night, reflecting on what the doctor has told him. By his side a green machine injects something, slowly, into his bloodstream. Kadafi serves his final customers wine and cigarettes from under the counter. Next door, the bar opens, puts out chairs and tables, turns up the volume, dims the lights.

Dawn

A black man with thick, thick spectacles sweeps the gutter with a green plastic broom. In Bamako his wife and children await the money order he will send from the post office on rue du Louvre, open all day Sunday for people such as him. In his bourgeois home the French president studies the timetable for the last days of his Presidential campaign.

The Kabyle sets La Mandoline coffee machine in motion and writes his luncheon menu.

A light wind moving between clouds and earth ruffles the early leaves on the plane trees. A blue neon 'Pompes Funèbres' sign is reflected in a puddle that is just the right length.

ACKNOWLEDGMENTS

Heartfelt thanks to friends, family and editors who've supported my work

'A day on the Rue du Faubourg', *The Cossack Review* (US).

'A parallel life',Kore Press Chapbook 2015. Winner Kore Press Short Story Award.

'Au pair girls wanted in France', *Orbis* (print) (UK), Irish Double Issue No. 69/70, Summer/Autumn 1988.

'Between men', *Sentinel Champions*, No.7.

'Frank stands his ground in Belleville', *Best Paris Stories* (print and ebook). Summertime publications (2012) anthology of prizewinning stories.

'I say "Good Morning" to my truck', *Crannóg* (Ireland) 14 (print), Spring 2007.

'I'm talking too much, aren't I?', *West 47* and *Cuirt Annual* 2005 print anthology (Ireland).

'It's not about the money', *Faber Book of Best New Irish Short Stories 2006-7* ed. David Marcus, Faber Books, London, 2007.

'Lightning strikes twice', *Southeast Review*, Vol.29, No.2 (print). Florida State University.

'Mastery', *Prick of the Spindle* (US) print magazine Issue 3.

'Musical Interlude', RTE Lyric FM July 2000.

'Nikodje's lap of honor', *Enigma* No.3 (print) (UK), Autumn 2009.

'Old wood best to burn', *Transnational Literature* (Australia) November 2013.

'Plugging the causal breach', *Numéro Cinq Magazine* May 2016

'Righteous Indignation', *Irish Times* 7 April 2001.

'What doesn't choke will fatten', *Prairie Schooner*, Spring 2012 (print). University of Nebraska Press.